Murder

and

Mozzarella

Michelle Ford

This is a work of fiction. Names, characters, places, and incidents either are the product of the author's imagination or are used factitiously, and any resemblance to any persons, living or dead, business establishments, events, or locales is entirely coincidental.

MURDER AND MOZZARELLA

All rights reserved.
Kinglet Books
Victoria BC, Canada
Copyright © 2022 Michelle Ford
Cover design by GetCovers

ISBN: 978-1989677483 (paperback)
ISBN: 978-1989677490 (ebook)
ISBN: 978-1989677506 (large print paperback)
ISBN: 978-1989677513 (hardcover)

No part of this book may be used or reproduced in any manner whatsoever without written permission from the author except in the case of brief quotations embodied in critical articles or reviews.

First edition: September 2022

Chapter 1

It was a hard call, but the first sniff of the day invariably belonged to the Roquefort.

"Hello, my blue beauty," Brianna West whispered when she opened the waxed paper wrapped around her favorite cheese. The package was still cold from the fridge where she stored most of her stock, including this Roquefort. Its pungent aroma featuring moldy socks and grass drifted deep into Brianna's nostrils when she inhaled, and a smile lifted her cheeks. "As fragrant as always. You're destined for pear and blue cheese Danish pastries today."

Brianna replaced the Roquefort and continued her morning tradition of sniffing each cheese currently in her fridge. She'd been doing this ritual since the industrial kitchen had been installed in her soon-to-be-open café. She'd determined that every item on the menu would feature cheese, which hadn't been a difficult decision. While she told anyone who asked that smelling the cheeses was an important part of assuring the freshest ingredients for her baked goods, she really did it because she adored cheese.

Her dairy products properly greeted, she pulled out a large bowl of risen dough from the fridge and a few blocks of butter then tied an apron over her jeans and striped blouse. She pulled her unruly mahogany curls into a no-nonsense ponytail that would keep it out of her way. Every recipe needed to be practiced and perfected before her grand opening. She had work to do.

Not that it might seem like terribly important work to someone other than her, she thought while she rolled the dough and cut it into squares for Danishes and sliced butter into a large bowl of flour. She'd been accustomed to her big city life in Vancouver, Canada, working as a consultant for small businesses and supporting her detective husband as he solved high-profile crimes. But when a bullet found her husband's carotid artery while undercover, she couldn't stay in her old life for a second longer. After a wine-soaked evening with her aunt Dot, she'd sold her condo in the city and, with the life insurance payout, bought a storefront on Driftwood Island where Dot lived.

Life was far too short to waste not following her passion. Cheese had always turned Brianna's good times into something close to divine, thanks to her sensitive nose and love of dairy from her grandmother. Now, she was merely weeks away from serving scones and pastries in her very own café, the Golden Moon. The biggest issues she had to solve these days were problems with her secondhand oven, although she was proud of herself for fixing the latest issue without calling a professional. If there were one thing she was good at, it was problem-solving.

Just as Brianna slid the last tray of scones into her temperamental oven, a knock rattled the door of the café beyond. It was too early for her carpenter to arrive, and Dot never rose before ten in the morning. Brianna poked her head into the café dining area to see who her visitor was.

Her heart squeezed every time she entered the cozy space of the Golden Moon. The café wasn't nearly ready for customers, but Brianna could see the future, and it looked like a wonderful dream. Swatches of paint on the drywall hinted at bright yellow walls to come. They were illuminated by tall frontage windows that gave the space a warm feel, enhanced by honey-stained hardwood floors and wooden farm-style chairs shoved in a corner. Brianna planned to sew cushions for each one using fabric printed with fanciful designs of cheese wheels. She had found vintage frames at a consignment store down the road and filled them with glossy photos of her favorite cheeses. They leaned against one wall, waiting to be affixed in place.

A box in the kitchen held a cluster of vintage cheese knives, which Brianna planned to artfully arrange in a pinwheel above the electric fireplace. If the décor and name didn't make the theme of the café clear enough, the counter display of cheesy baked goods would satisfy any lingering curiosity. The counter wasn't built yet—her carpenter would be hard at work on that project today—but Brianna had an excellent imagination.

Brianna brightened at the sight of her childhood friend at the glass door. She and Macy Jones had drifted apart after high school on the larger Victoria Island—Brianna to university in the mainland city of Vancouver where she'd met her late husband, and a teenage Macy raising her unplanned daughter on Driftwood Island where her grandparents lived—but Brianna had tried hard to reconnect after moving back. They now had a tentative but swiftly warming friendship.

Brianna bustled to the door and let Macy in. Her friend's bright smile under her shoulder-length blond hair and bangs was infectious. Grinning, Brianna unlocked the door and ushered Macy through.

"Well, hello, hello, my baking bosom buddy," Macy said. She straightened her demure blouse, clearly on her way to work at the nearby preschool. "I won't be in your way for long, I know you're busy practicing your baking. Wow, something smells great. What am I saying? It always smells great in here. I swear I've gained five pounds since you've started trialing recipes."

"I aim to please." Brianna walked toward the kitchen, where she'd already set up the café's espresso machine. Just because the café's counter wasn't yet installed didn't mean Brianna couldn't drink quality beverages. She called to Macy over her shoulder, "Coffee?"

"Does a duck swim?"

Brianna grabbed a mug and placed it under the nozzle. She peeked her head around the corner. "Double shot, extra vanilla?"

"You remembered." Macy beamed at her, and the warmth in Brianna's stomach reminded her of why she'd moved here. It was good to be back. Vancouver, for all its excitement, had never truly felt like home. Driftwood Island wasn't where she'd grown up—she'd lived in nearby Nanaimo on the larger Victoria Island—but she'd visited her aunt here often enough, and Macy's familiar face made the island comfortable in a way Vancouver had never been.

After the machine's requisite noise, Brianna walked

back into the unfinished dining area with two mugs and passed the fragrant coffee to her old friend. Macy took a dainty sip then held the mug in both hands for warmth.

"I noticed your help wanted ad in the window," she said, blowing on her drink.

Brianna waved at the counter. "There's a lot to do. When the café opens, I'll be too busy baking and running the till and cleaning up all by myself. I'd love someone for the front counter so I can focus on baking. We'll see. My flyer hasn't had any bites yet."

"About that." Macy straightened her spine and stared at Brianna with hope in her eyes. "Would you consider hiring Oaklyn? She's in the market for a part-time job, weekends and after school. She works hard when she puts her mind to it."

Brianna sighed inwardly. She'd already heard rumors about Macy's teenaged daughter Oaklyn being a troublemaker. One story even had Oaklyn—allegedly—shoving fireworks in a Halloween pumpkin, which had sprayed the front of the irate neighbor's house with bits of squash. When Brianna had met Oaklyn last month for the first time in years, her first impression hadn't put the rumors to rest. Dyed, spiky black hair, far too much eyeliner, and a bored-at-everything expression hadn't endeared Oaklyn to Brianna.

But money was always tight with Macy. She'd had to raise Oaklyn on her own for all these years, and that included paying for night college for Macy to get her early childhood educator diploma. If Oaklyn could fund her own extras, it would give her mother a much-needed break from being sole-breadwinner. And Macy was her friend. Brianna couldn't say no to the hope in her eyes.

"Of course," Brianna said with far more enthusiasm than she felt. Afternoons and weekends would help, but she'd have to find someone else to come in the mornings too. Brianna could make it work for now. "Let's give her a trial run. Grand opening is in two weeks. Have her come in on the Friday evening before then, and I'll show her the ropes."

Macy's face relaxed with a relieved smile. "Thanks. She'll be great. You won't regret this."

Brianna wasn't so sure about that, but she could bear a lot to make Macy smile.

Brianna's head twisted toward an odd clopping sound coming from the window. Macy gasped, and coffee sloshed out of her mug and onto her sensible pants.

"Drat!" Macy slammed the mug onto a nearby pile of wood and brushed at the stain with ineffectual sweeps of her hands. "I need to move my car. It's parked illegally."

"You need to do it now?" Brianna stared at her friend while she tossed her a rag the carpenter had left lying around.

"Yes, yes," she said, diving into her purse for keys. "He's coming. I can't afford a ticket right now."

Brianna frowned at Macy's cryptic words. Who was 'he'? In the face of Macy's distress, there was only one thing to do. She swiped Macy's keys from her friend's hand and walked toward the door.

"I'll move the car," she called over her shoulder. "You get cleaned up."

The clopping sound stopped. Brianna hustled out the door, curious to discover the source of Macy's angst. Her friend's tiny red hatchback was parked in front of the café's alley where Brianna's bicycle sat next to the neighboring yarn shop. It was early enough that few other cars were parked along this side street of Snuggler's Cove, the only town on Driftwood Island. Brianna tucked her hands into her pockets to avoid an early morning breeze that cooled the summer sun. Beside Macy's car was a sight that had Brianna blinking.

Chapter 2

A tall horse with a shiny black coat stood patiently beside the hatchback. Astride the animal was a strikingly handsome man with broad shoulders and a strong jaw. He wore well-ironed dark blue pants with gold striping and a police cap, which meant he must be a member of the Royal Canadian Mounted Police who dealt with law enforcement on Driftwood Island. He sat tall on the horse with ease, as if he rode the animal often. His dark brows were contracted as he scribbled on a notepad.

"You're an unexpected sight," Brianna said, trying to hide the chuckle in her voice. "Can I help you, officer?"

"Is this your car?" He pointed at the hatchback then waved at an elderly lady passing behind the vehicle.

"I was just about to move it." Brianna smiled winningly at the Mountie. "I own the café, so no harm done."

"It's illegally parked," he informed her.

Brianna managed not to roll her eyes, but it was difficult. Was crime so nonexistent on the island that parking infractions were what occupied the local constabulary? The island was small, but the population still numbered in the thousands. She wasn't in the city anymore, that was for certain.

A thread of disquiet wove through her mind. City life wasn't hers any longer. How could she berate this man for dealing with petty issues when her focus these days was baking cheese pastries?

"I'll move it right now," Brianna said. "I promise it won't happen again."

The Mountie stared at her for a moment, then he ripped the parking ticket in two.

"Good," he said. "As long as this is the only time." He glanced at the café, newly hung with a yellow and white striped awning. The words "The Golden Moon" were emblazoned in black lettering across the window. "This is new. You're the owner, you said?"

"Brianna West." She considered sticking out her hand, but he was perched so far above her on his horse that it seemed ridiculous to try.

"Corporal Devon Moore," he replied.

An awkward pause ensued, then Brianna blurted out the question that plagued her. "I have to ask, what's with the horse? I know you're a Mountie, but I kind of thought the horse thing was a relic of an older time."

"It is." He patted the horse's mane with a genuine smile. "Sarge here is retired and living his golden years on the West Coast. But he still needs exercise, so I take him out every few days."

A loud ripping noise resounded in the quiet street. Brianna chuckled, and the horse flicked his ears. Corporal Moore's eyes widened, then he tried to cover his embarrassment with a shrug.

"He's been working hard," he said. "That's what happens."

"Would he like a carrot?" Brianna asked. She rubbed the horse's soft nose, and Sarge pushed gently against her hand.

"I don't think I've ever seen him refuse one."

Brianna ran into the café and through to the kitchen. Macy must have been cleaning up in the bathroom because the café was empty. After a deep sniff of scone-scented air, Brianna grabbed her oven mitts and pulled out her tray. The scones were perfectly golden with crisp edges of cooked cheese, and Brianna's mouth watered. She rummaged in the fridge for a carrot destined for carrot cake with cream cheese icing, wrapped a fresh scone in a napkin, and raced back outside before Corporal Moore could rethink Macy's parking ticket.

"For you, Sarge." Brianna offered the carrot to the horse, who wrapped floppy lips around the treat. Loud crunching told Brianna that her offering was satisfactory. She reached up to Sarge's rider. "And for you. Careful, it's hot."

Corporal Moore reached for the napkin. When their fingers touched, heat rose in Brianna's stomach. She squashed the unnerving sensation down firmly, surprised at herself. Here she was, a widow of only six months, and she was already interested in the first good-looking man who made contact?

He brought the napkin to his lap and stared at the scone in his hands. "Thank you." He glanced at Brianna with a shrewd look in his chocolate-brown eyes. "But don't think I don't know what this is."

"What?" Brianna tried to look innocent.

"You're trying to butter me up, so I won't mark you down for future parking tickets. It won't work." Corporal Moore bit into the scone, then his eyes closed. "Mmm. Well, it probably won't work. I do appreciate you trying, though."

Macy came out of the bathroom as Brianna shut the café door behind her. Her black pants were slightly darker on one leg, but otherwise her spill was unnoticeable.

"Did you make it in time?" she asked. "I swear, that man is a stickler for rules. Almost five thousand people live on Driftwood, but maybe that's still too small, or else he's following me around to watch for violations. I don't know whether to be annoyed or flattered. He's incredibly attractive, so I'll err on the side of flattery for now. But I really can't afford a ticket."

"You could park legally," Brianna suggested, her mouth twisting as she suppressed her smile. "Just a suggestion."

Macy huffed a laugh. "Yes, but then I'd have to walk an extra block, and I wouldn't have time for coffee with you before I get to work, would I?"

Brianna raised her mug, and the two women clinked their cups and drank.

"Where did Devon Moore come from, anyway?" Brianna asked. She was curious about a new face on the island, that was all. She had no other reason for learning more about the handsome Mountie, none whatsoever. "I thought I'd met all the officials when I applied for a building permit at the municipal office."

"That's because he's been away for the past month." Macy reached into her purse for her lipstick. "Taking care of his sick mother on the mainland, at least that's what I heard through the grapevine. He's only lived on the island since Christmas, though. He took the job after Perkins retired from the force. Opinions are divided on what sort of man he is. The older set seem to think of him as an upstanding gentleman, and I know Magnus Pickleton from the marina has taken him out fishing once or twice. Devon mainly keeps to himself, although Cecilia from the post office would love to get her claws in him, no doubt. She's been trying, a little too hard, you know." Macy pushed her lips together in a pout. "Oh, Corporal Moore, you must be so lonely in your cabin on the lake."

Brianna chuckled, imagining the confusion and disdain that would surely cross Devon Moore's face at the unknown Cecilia's antics.

"Oh, to be a fly on the wall during that exchange," she said.

Macy slung her purse over her shoulder. "I'd better be off. The children await."

"How is the preschool? Do you still enjoy the work?"

Macy's face lit up. "I adore those little snot monsters. They are such a joy. I don't mean to brag—okay, maybe I do—but I have a way with them. Even the little terrors calm down with me. Firm but gentle, that's my strategy. They know where they're at with me." Her happy expression grew pensive. "I only wish we could provide more extras. We don't charge a lot—our families tend to be the more disadvantaged ones on the island—so our budgets aren't huge. Government subsidies help, but the funds we get keep us running and that's it."

"What kind of extras are you hoping for?"

"Art supplies would be amazing." Macy held up her hands and wiggled them. "Finger painting is the best, and drawing, all that. But consumables get used up quickly, and there's never enough to go around."

Brianna drummed her fingers on the table, an idea quickly coalescing in her mind.

"What if," she said slowly, "I donated all profits from my grand opening to your preschool, earmarked for art supplies for the kids?"

Macy's eyes grew wide. "You'd do that?"

"It's not entirely selfless," Brianna admitted. "I could use the extra promo. But yeah, I'd love to see the profits go toward a worthy cause like that. What do you think?"

"I think the preschool and I have some advertising to do." Macy grinned. "Give me some flyers, and I'll go nuts."

Macy took her phone out of her purse. Her eyes widened. "Shoot, I have to go. I'll be late for work at this rate. Some parents take the early drop-off time a little too seriously and get pretty riled up if I'm a minute late for their cherubs. Old Hilda Button from the Bumblebee Bed and Breakfast is usually the first with her granddaughter, but she's so sweet. She just likes to chat with everyone who turns up."

She swooped in for a hug, which Brianna gratefully returned. Although she and Greg hadn't been on the best of terms before he'd died, still, a decade of embraces had trained her body to expect closeness. Now that she was on her own, she appreciated Macy's spontaneous hugs.

Macy blew her a kiss and rushed off, and Brianna returned to the kitchen. Her carpenter Shaun Bartley would arrive shortly, and she liked to give him free rein of the café without her skulking in the back. She didn't need to hear about every little mistake he made and subsequently fixed. Ignorance was often bliss. She had plenty of paperwork to do at her float home. Baking was only a small part of starting a bakery-café, she'd found out.

Chapter 3

The next Tuesday, Brianna packaged another batch of cooled scones and Danishes in a large tin with a floral pattern, tidied the kitchen counters, ran the dishwasher through a cycle, and let herself out the side door. Her treat tin fit inside the wire basket at the back of her bicycle perfectly, and she threw her leg over the frame and pushed into the street.

Traffic was still light at this hour—although "heavy" traffic in Snuggler's Cove was anything more than three cars in a row—and she peacefully passed a stretch of quaint shops that lined the road hugging a small inlet. A wide walkway clung to the top of a seawall between road and ocean, and colorful umbrellas cast shade onto arriving ice cream vendors and artists selling their wares.

Brianna pumped her bike pedals up the last steep hill toward her aunt's house. Signs for a cidery flashed by, and a flock of placid sheep watched her pass as they chewed grass in a rolling field lined by verdant conifers.

She crested the hill, briefly overtaken by a rusty pickup truck with bumper stickers calling for peace and coexistence. A bucolic scene greeted Brianna's eyes once the truck trundled past and her tired legs slowed on the downhill. A narrow valley bordered on both sides by dense forest gave way to gently rolling hills dotted with sheep and bisected with bright white fences. Barns clustered at each farmstead, and leafy maples and oaks waved in the fresh breeze flowing in from the ocean at the end of the valley.

Brianna whizzed down the steep incline, and her cheeks lifted in a grin at her speed. She'd done this exact ride many times as a teenager, and she'd forgotten how good it felt to let go and let gravity take over. She worried briefly that she wouldn't be able to handle herself if her bike flew over an unexpected bump, but joy soon pushed doubts out of her mind.

Too soon, the hill was conquered, and Brianna pedaled into her aunt's gravel driveway lined with white fence boards that meandered in a curving fashion to the red farmhouse she'd spent many happy summers visiting. A wide swing on the wraparound porch beckoned her to relax on its cushioned seat, and large windows let so much light into the house that Brianna could see straight through to the back garden. Trim painted a striking black encircled every window.

Brianna leaned her bike against the stair railing and glanced westward. A large excavator sat silent in the neighbor's field, next to a winding creek that meandered through the property and spilled into a pond on Dot's land. Nothing had been dug yet, and Brianna wondered what the plan was while she climbed three shallow steps to the porch. A ripped and stained bike trailer sat on the ground beside the stairs, and a large ceramic elephant stared at her with sleepy eyes from its post beside the door. She patted its head just as she'd done as a teenager. Then she knocked on the shiny black door, the bold color choices perfectly reflecting the woman who lived here.

No one answered. Brianna frowned and knocked louder. She tried the door, and it swung open.

Her aunt's familiar living room met her eyes. Walls painted a rich terracotta were mostly covered by an excess of framed photographs of exotic locales, taken by Dot on her travels. A massive painted fan hung over sliding doors leading to the back deck, vases and figurines perched on every available surface, and a chandelier of mirrors and colored glass hung in pride of place above the dining table. Large, embroidered cushions clashed magnificently with colorful throws on the couches, and a Turkish rug lent the room a cozy feeling that tied the glut of decorations together. It was a chaos that brought Brianna fond memories.

"Hello?" Brianna called out, but the house was silent and still. She walked to a set of sliding glass doors along the back wall and opened them to better examine the back yard. A wall of trees encroached a carefully tended vegetable patch filled with flowering peas and blades of garlic.

A flash of fuchsia caught Brianna's eyes, and her heart leaped. Her aunt emerged from the forest path, a flowing peasant shirt in the riotous hue making her hard to miss. Her short, fluffy hair, blond and white mixed together, waved with the motion of her steps.

Dot Dubois was her father's younger sister and was the wild one in the family. She'd spent her youth traveling and getting into trouble in all reaches of the world. She would come home long enough to make money to travel again. Brianna had loved hearing her aunt's strange, exotic tales of adventure and discovery.

She could remember asking her aunt to repeat the story of her elephant ride through the jungles of Laos again and again. It was only when Brianna was a teenager that Dot had told her the darker stories, like the time she'd spent a month in a Peruvian jail for some crime she hadn't confessed to Brianna.

Dot had eventually slowed her wandering ways, taking up with an investor she'd met in the Philippines while he was sailing solo around the world. They married and continued to sail, with an occasional foray back to Canada. The ensuing divorce five years later had set Dot up with enough cash to buy land on Driftwood Island. It was an odd choice for a wandering soul, but Brianna supposed that people changed. Brianna had given up her big-city life to become a café owner on the same small island, an event she never would have predicted six months ago.

Brianna called out a greeting and waved at her aunt. Dot nearly leaped out of her gumboots at the sound, but she recovered quickly and waved back an enthusiastic welcome. When Dot clomped up the stairs, her muddy harem pants swishing around sturdy legs, Brianna hugged her tightly. Dot heaved for breath like she'd been running.

"It's good to see you, child," Dot said, brushing Brianna's hair in the affectionate way she always had. "I wasn't expecting you."

"What were you doing?" Brianna stood back and looked at her aunt's bedraggled pants, muddy up to the knees, and her heaving chest. "You look like you ran here through a pig's mud pit."

Dot clutched a hand to her chest and laughed the deep belly laugh that Brianna found so infectious. She put hands on her ample stomach with a grin. "Maybe I did. I need to work off those scones you're always bringing around. Maybe mud pit running is my new exercise regime. I'm a trendsetter, you know. It'll be the next big thing, mark my words."

"I'll stick to bike riding, thank you. Hey, are you still sailing these days?" Dot had used to take a younger Brianna out on her tiny sailing dinghy, and the two of them had bonded many times over knots, harbor seals, and rogue gusts of wind. Greg had never been interested in taking the sport up with Brianna in Vancouver, so she'd allowed her skills to lapse. Being surrounded by glittering ocean on Driftwood Island had rekindled Brianna's desire.

"Yes, the good ship Guster." Dot smiled in recollection. "We had some wild times on that little cork, didn't we? I haven't taken her out yet this year, but I'd love to get her in the water with you. The poor thing is probably pining for a sail."

"It's a date." Brianna held out her tin of baked goods. "I have some more treats for you to sample, since you've earned them with all that mud running. And I want your honest opinion."

"I'm always honest with my opinions." Dot chuckled and walked into the house, Brianna following. "But we'll need tea to go with them. I'll put the kettle on."

"What's with the excavator on the neighbor's property?" Brianna asked. "I can't remember who lives there now."

Dot shoved her kettle under the faucet and twisted the tap with force until water hissed out in a violent flow.

"Don't get me started on Owen and his plans." Dot glared out the window toward her neighbor's house. Her mood had switched from pleasant to scowling in an instant, but Brianna was used to her aunt's mercurial nature. "Blooming Owen Montague, mister high and mighty himself, God's gift to womankind, the owner of Driftwood Island's first herd of water buffalo, has decided to redirect the stream into the storm drain at the road."

"You mean the creek that fills your pond?" Brianna frowned. "That can't be legal."

"That pond supports a rich diversity of life, not to mention it's where I get water for the garden and Zola." Dot turned the water off and slammed the kettle onto the stove. "And trust me, I've tried the legal route, but as long as the township approves, I don't have a leg to stand on. And guess what? Owen the schmoozer has friends in the council. Must be nice to have deep pockets." Dot stamped her foot and raised her hands to mimic strangling someone. "I could just murder that sanctimonious, hypocritical bastard."

"I'm so sorry to hear that." Brianna grabbed a plate from the cupboard and dished out a few scones and Danishes. She didn't believe that nothing could be done, although it wasn't in Dot's nature to give up too easily. Brianna had inherited her own stubborn streak from that side of the family. "I can help you look into it if you like. There must be something we can do."

"You're a sweet one." Dot squeezed her shoulder.

"Thank you. I think I've explored all avenues, but I'm happy to have a second pair of eyes. Oh!" Dot's eyes grew round. "I forgot, Zola is still wandering around the south pasture. I meant to move her this morning. She'll be chewing the fence soon, there's so little grass for her. Would you be a doll and take her to the west field? I ought to change my pants into something cleaner for our teatime."

Brianna nodded and walked out the front door into the brilliant sunshine. Three pairs of gumboots in various sizes lounged beside the ceramic elephant, and Brianna kicked off her sandals and slipped into her favorite pair that were yellow with purple polka dots. Her aunt always had a few spare boots for guests, since her fields were often muddy on the rainy West Coast.

The only muck Brianna had to worry about on this sunny late spring day was produced by Zola, Dot's pet goat. Dot pretended she was a farmer, but Brianna knew better. Zola wasn't milked, shorn, or asked to produce kids. Zola was Dot's pet, and the goat knew her exalted place.

Brianna strode to a gate in the fence that lined the driveway and creaked its wobbly wooden frame open wide. At the edge of the small pasture, the grass trimmed short and an unidentifiable bush in the center denuded of leaves, stood a miniature white goat. Her slitted eyes gazed at Brianna with an intelligence that she knew only too well. Zola was a master at escaping her bonds, and Brianna was only surprised that the goat was still in this pasture.

"Hi, Zola," she said. "Ready to move? Let's go."

Zola's eyes glanced at the open gate. With nonchalance, she slowly ambled toward Brianna. Just before Brianna could reach out to grab Zola's halter, the little goat nimbly sidestepped, trotted around her, and slipped out the gate.

"Zola!" Brianna shouted, but the goat was off, leaping westward. Brianna gave chase as the goat skirted fences, dashed around a small barn that housed hay and Zola during the winter, and behind a tiny tractor. Brianna raced after the runaway goat, her heart pounding with exertion. That same heart dropped in her chest when Zola wriggled under a loose piece of wire fencing that separated Dot's land from the neighbor's.

Once Zola passed through the breach, she stood straight, shook her tail with a fussy gesture, then trotted off in search of new adventures. Brianna cursed and shoved her foot between strands of wire to rest on fence boards. She couldn't let Zola run amok on the neighbor's property. Five minutes in a vegetable patch, and any produce would be decimated. She'd seen it happen at her aunt's. Zola was voracious and ate anything and everything.

Brianna heaved herself over the fence, ripping a hole in her jeans as she did so, and landed with a wobble on the other side. Grass gave way to a gravel driveway. A pickup truck and a small gray sedan were parked outside a farmhouse covered in tidy white siding. A high peaked roof rose over a covered porch at the front with one lounge chair sprawled on the side. Azalea bushes lined the front in a trim row of hedging. Brianna hoped that the residents weren't watching her trespass, even if it were for a good cause. Her aunt clearly wasn't on the best of terms with the family there, and she didn't want to escalate any troubles between them.

She turned to where Zola had disappeared. A large barn door yawned open, its cavernous interior dark despite the sunshine outside. She stepped cautiously into the dim, dusty space, her eyes searching for the white of Zola's coat.

"Zola?" she called out quietly. The barn was too hushed to shout. "Zola, are you in here?"

A rustling made Brianna jump, but it was only the goat. She trotted toward Brianna and nuzzled her hand.

"Oh, now you're going to come quietly, are you?" Brianna bent down to rub the goat's head then laced her fingers through the animal's halter. Now that her eyes were growing used to the lack of light, features of the barn emerged in the gloom. Stalls for horses and cows lined one side—empty now that the animals were pastured outside for the summer—and stacks of hay filled the other side. The central area was likely stored with tractors and other equipment during the winter months, but right now the empty space was occupied by only one thing. Brianna's fingers tightened on Zola's halter.

A body lay face down on the ground, a pitchfork stuck into its back.

Chapter 4

Brianna froze, her body numb as horror seeped slowly into every corner of her mind. She had no doubt the person was dead. No one could get a pitchfork stabbed in their back and live to tell the tale.

Once the initial wave of horror passed over her and receded, Brianna's heart stopped galloping in her chest and resumed an almost normal pace. She had seen worse in the gory crime dramas her late detective husband had loved to watch and gleefully pick apart for inaccurate details. She was no stranger to death. Greg had seen to that.

She backed slowly away, careful not to disturb the scene any more than she and Zola already had. The body's head faced the door, and she avoided looking at the man's wide, staring eyes and instead traced the cord of music earbuds flopped across his pale cheek. The pitchfork had very slender tines with presumably sharp ends, she noted with a detached eye that refused to think too hard about what the implement was stabbed into. But no matter how sharp the tines, not even the clumsiest person could manage to fall on a pitchfork backward. This was murder, clear and simple.

Once the body left her range of sight, she took a deep, calming breath and rummaged in her pocket for her phone. With trembling fingers, she dialed the emergency number.

A beep indicated that she had no signal. She cursed and whirled around, but no signal bars miraculously appeared on her screen. Coverage on the island was notoriously spotty, and her aunt had often complained about a dead zone at her place.

Brianna stifled a manic giggle. The words "dead zone" were a little too on-the-nose today. She sobered and shoved her phone back in her pocket. The authorities needed to know about the dead man in the barn. Her eyes locked on the farmhouse nearby. Surely the occupants would have a landline. They were closer than Dot's place.

Brianna's stomach clenched. They were probably family to the man in the barn. Was he Owen Montague, Dot's hated neighbor? Would she have to break the news of his murder to his family? What if they were the murderers? She needed to get back to Dot's house to call the police.

She squared her shoulders, grabbed Zola's collar more firmly in her shaking fingers, and marched toward the fence.

Her steps slowed as she passed the house. An ornamental metal sign tucked into a flowerpot of petunias beside the door stated, "My son is my sun," with a painted sunflower drooping over the words. Brianna was too busy reading the sign to notice the front door opening.

"Who are you?" A shrill voice called out. "What are you doing on our property?"

A short, compact woman with a neat bob of dyed-blond hair stood inside, sucking on the straw of a takeaway smoothie cup in pastel stripes of green and pink. Her rounded frame was covered in a bloody apron. The red streaks turned Brianna's stomach. The woman's sharp blue eyes shifted from Brianna to Zola, to the yard beyond, then back to Brianna.

"Well?" she demanded in her high voice. Brianna could imagine her either singing a sweet lullaby or shouting shrilly across the yard. "Are you selling something?" Her eyes rested on Zola. The goat shifted her hooves and reached her mouth toward the flowers. Brianna pulled her away. The woman continued, "We're in the middle of butchering some chickens, so speak up or leave, please."

Brianna sighed with relief at the explanation of the apron's red stains. After seeing a dead body and worrying that the farmhouse inhabitants might be the culprits, blood immediately brought death and murder to mind.

"I'm Brianna West," she explained. "Your neighbor Dot's niece."

"I'm Tansy Montague," the woman said. "Is there a reason you're here? I really should get back to the chickens."

"My aunt's goat ran off," Brianna said. "I came over to fetch her, and I followed her into your barn. That's where I saw—" Brianna gulped. What was the proper protocol for telling someone about a murder? Greg hadn't ever explained that topic. "A man, lying on the ground. He had a pitchfork sticking out of his back. He's dead. We need to call the police."

The woman stared at her and blinked three times in succession.

"No," she whispered. She released her drink from limp fingers, and it toppled to the ground with a splat of thick, peach-colored liquid. She fumbled at her apron strings and ripped the garment off her head. It dropped to the floor as Tansy brushed past Brianna in a run. She tossed a yell over her shoulder. "Jay, come to the barn. Quickly!"

Brianna followed with reluctance. She knew the man in the barn was beyond saving, and Tansy deserved a moment alone with what might be her husband.

Then Brianna frowned and sped up. This was a murder scene. She couldn't let Tansy muck up any evidence that might be lying around. She broke into a run, and Zola bleated as she dragged the goat behind her.

"Tansy," Brianna shouted at the barn door. "Don't touch anything. The police will need evidence."

Tansy knelt at the body's side, carefully out of the pool of blood that had soaked into straw on the concrete floor. Her shoulders shook with loud sobs.

"Owen," she yelled out, her words thick with anguished tears. "Owen?" She looked up at Brianna through red eyes and fought for breath. "Who would do this? I don't understand."

"I'm so sorry for your loss," Brianna said. Zola tried to nibble on her shirt hem, and Brianna held the goat away from her body as far as her arms would allow. "But please, come away from the scene. The cleaner we can keep the barn, the easier the police will find the killer."

At the word "killer", Tansy broke into fresh sobs, but she rose unsteadily and stumbled toward the door. A shadow darkened the straw at her feet, and Brianna turned around.

A young man, his face drained of color, stared in horror at the body. His wispy, light-brown hair lifted in the breeze as if wanting to escape the scene. Despite the pale waxiness of the dead man's complexion, the resemblance between Owen and this younger man was clear. Was this Tansy and the dead Owen's son? If so, the son had inherited his father's coloring and build, although he'd missed out on the strong features of the dead man, instead presenting a milder, weak-chinned version. His mother threw herself into the young man's arms with a renewal of heaving sobs.

"Jay, he's dead," Tansy forced out. She wailed anew. "Someone killed him."

Jay clutched his mother, unable to tear his eyes away from his father's body. Gently, Brianna touched his shoulder to turn his eyes away from the gruesome sight.

"Do you have a land line?" she asked. "We need to call the police."

Jay blinked at Brianna as if wondering who she was. Then he nodded, pushed his mother gently away, then trudged back to the farmhouse.

Brianna tugged Zola's halter when the goat stepped toward the body, the animal's natural curiosity overcoming any aversion to death. Tansy's breath calmed, and she opened her streaming eyes to look again on her husband's form.

"That's not our pitchfork," Tansy said with a hard edge to her voice. "I've never painted a tool like that."

Brianna glanced at the pitchfork. She hadn't noticed before—the dead body was rather distracting—but the pitchfork's wooden handle was painted a brilliant red. Up and down the length sprouted polka dots of black and white. A sinking feeling threatened to overwhelm Brianna's already beleaguered nerves with dread.

"That's Dot Dubois's pitchfork," Tansy said in a hushed voice.

Chapter 5

Brianna glanced at Tansy. The other woman breathed heavily and stared at the pitchfork. Then she turned to Brianna.

"Who did this?" she screeched. Her already high voice reached a stratospheric pitch. "You said you're Dot's niece. What were you doing here?"

"Chasing this goat." Brianna pointed at Zola with her free hand. "And why on Earth would I kill your husband? I don't know him or you."

Tansy stared at Brianna, her eyes raking her face. Then she ran a hand over her forehead.

"Maybe so," she muttered. "But this is Dot's pitchfork."

"Yoo-hoo," a familiar voice sang out from outside the barn. "Brianna, are you there?"

Brianna squeezed her eyes tight. Dot's presence here wouldn't help anyone.

Sure enough, Tansy whirled around, her eyes wide. "You!" she screamed. "You, you—murderer!"

Dot stopped outside the barn door with her eyebrows drawn together. Then she caught sight of Owen in the barn, and her breath caught.

"What happened?" she whispered.

"Why are you pretending to be shocked?" Tansy screamed. "You murdered Owen! It's your pitchfork in his back." She dropped to her knees and began wailing again. "What did he ever do to you that would make you kill him?"

Dot didn't acknowledge Tansy's tirade, nor did she look at Brianna. She merely stared at Owen's body, a host of thoughts flitting through her eyes.

"Dot?" Brianna said quietly. "Did you lend someone your pitchfork?"

Unbidden, Dot's words came back to Brianna. *I could just murder that sanctimonious, hypocritical bastard.* Dot had been angry, almost beyond reason. She and Owen had bad blood, that was certain. Could it have been enough for Dot to snap?

No. Brianna couldn't believe it of her loving aunt. She wasn't capable of such an act of hate. Brianna bit her lip. Although Dot had been in plenty of trouble with the law in her past. But murder, that was a whole different story. And would she really have said those words *after* killing Owen in earnest?

"I often lean it against the shared fence behind my barn," Dot said faintly, still not looking at Brianna. "It's where I park my wheelbarrow."

"Dot didn't kill Owen," Brianna said out loud to convince both Tansy and herself of her aunt's innocence. "There's no way."

"Then how do you explain the pitchfork?" Tansy hissed, her eyes bright. "And what do you know, anyway? You hardly know your aunt. You moved here from the city. You don't know anything about our ways here. Keep your nose out of this."

Brianna recoiled. Tansy's words mimicked Greg's in spirit, if not in language. Her late husband had frequently berated her for her attempts to help him with his cases. "You have no idea how all this works," he'd said to her with a tug of her hair to soften the impact of his words. "You keep your pretty little nose where it belongs."

"I know her well enough for this," Brianna retorted. "And I was with her just before now. Dot, tell her where you were before I came over. Let's clear all this up."

Dot was silent, still staring at Owen as if the body would roll over and walk once more. Brianna waited for her aunt to say something, anything, to clear suspicion from her name. Why was she silent? Had Owen's death affected her that much?

"It was either you or Brianna here," Tansy said, pointing a shaking finger at Brianna. "One of you stabbed my poor, sweet husband, I know it."

"It wasn't Brianna." Dot finally tore her eyes away from Owen and fixed them on Tansy with a reproving stare. "She didn't even know Owen."

Brianna's heart warmed. Dot had seemed almost catatonic over the murder, but she'd roused herself enough to defend her niece.

"Then it was you." Jay's voice cracked on the last word. He strode into view and stood next to his mother. He hauled her upright and wrapped a protective arm around her shoulder. "The police will be here any minute. You'd better not go anywhere."

"Dot isn't the killer," Brianna said, growing exasperated by the accusations flying around. This wasn't due process. It was a witch hunt. "Let the police sort it out."

"How are you defending her?" Jay's voice dripped

with incredulity.

"Don't blame Brianna for wanting to find the truth," Dot said with her hands on her hips.

"Find the 'truth' you want her to find, you mean," Tansy cried out. "We'll see what the police have to say about it. I hear them coming now."

Sure enough, sirens wailed in the distance. Brianna glanced at Dot, whose eyes had slid back to Owen as if magnetized. Something in her expression had changed. Had shock given way to determination? Brianna twined her fingers more securely into Zola's halter. What did her aunt mean to do?

"We're in the barn," Tansy screamed when the sirens stopped and the sound of car doors slamming filtered through the barn's wooden walls. "We have the murderer!"

Brianna blinked as Devon Moore came around the corner of the barn, closely followed by another officer, a lanky older man with a long face and large, soulful eyes. Both newcomers sized up the situation quickly.

"Step away from the body," Devon said to the group. "I'm a police officer, and anything you say may be given in evidence."

When the others shuffled out of the wide barn doors, Devon knelt next to Owen and pressed his fingertips to the dead man's neck. The other officer surveyed the area, checking for danger. After a moment, Devon released his hold and sat back on his heels, surveying the scene.

"He's gone," he said quietly.

"Of course he is," Tansy whispered. "You think I didn't check? Look at him. He's cold."

She buried her face in her son's chest, and Jay glared at Devon. Devon stood and sighed.

"Call for back-up, Lenox," he said to the lanky Mountie. "This is a murder investigation now. And you four." He looked at Brianna and the others. "I'll need to take you in for questioning."

"No need, officer." Dot stepped forward, her chin held high. "I did it. I stabbed Owen in the back with my own pitchfork."

Brianna's gasp was barely audible over Tansy's exclamation.

"She confessed," Tansy said, her eyes wide and disbelieving. Her shaking finger pointed at Dot, who didn't meet Tansy's stare. "That's the woman who murdered my husband. She's standing right there. Get her!"

Devon exchanged an incredulous glance with Lennox, although his hands fumbled at his belt for a pair of handcuffs that dangled there.

"I am arresting you for the murder of this man." He looked at Tansy for a name. Brianna remembered that Devon had only lived in Smuggler's Cove for a few months before her, and the island was large enough that not everyone immediately knew everyone.

"Owen Montague," Tansy choked out. "My husband. That's Dot Dubois, our neighbor."

Devon looked to Dot for confirmation, and she nodded.

"This is ridiculous," Brianna burst out. "What are you doing, Dot? You didn't kill Owen."

Did you? was the unspoken question that Brianna left

dangling in the air. She didn't understand. Dot was many things—wandering, wise, wild, and willful—but a killer? Sure, she could get worked into a passion, but stabbing a neighbor with a pitchfork was a stretch.

"I killed Owen." Dot's assuredness grew with every repetition of her confession. She held out her wrists toward Devon. "It's always the people closest to the victim, isn't it? And I'm his neighbor. It's no secret that we've been at each other's throats for years. I finally got the last word, that's all."

Dot had never been a callous woman, and her words struck Brianna as false. But after Dot's confession, what could Brianna do? She watched as Devon recited a litany of charter rights and warnings then clicked the handcuffs over her aunt's wrists. Dot stared straight ahead and followed the Mounties when they led her toward their vehicle.

Before Dot slipped into the backseat of the car, she finally met Brianna's eyes.

"I did it, Brianna," she said clearly. "I know you, you'll want to find out more. But there's nothing to find except my guilt, so let it be. Open your café and move on with your life."

She allowed Lenox to guide her head into the car. Brianna's throat thickened as the car's tires crunched on the gravel driveway. How had she woken up this morning in a good mood? How was the sun still shining?

Brianna's eyes narrowed. Dot was right: she wanted to find out more. She knew her aunt. The woman trapped spiders in the house to release them outside, even if they found their way back in the next night. She was a stalwart vegetarian, mainly because she couldn't stand the thought of an animal dying for her benefit. Dot's confession stretched credulity, and Brianna wasn't buying Dot's act. Something else was going on here. Blackmail? Threats? Something more sinister? Brianna had an excellent nose for both cheese and liars, and she smelled a big moldy lie in this barnyard.

Chapter 6

More police arrived and took Brianna and the others to the station to be questioned about their whereabouts that morning. Before they left, Brianna dragged Zola back to Dot's pasture on a makeshift lead that she'd commandeered from the barn. Given that Dot had confessed to the crime, Brianna wasn't under suspicion, but the police wanted to know details of how she'd found Owen and what Dot had been up to before Brianna had discovered the body.

Brianna didn't have great answers for them. Every detail that she remembered about Dot—her breathless arrival covered in mud, her threats to Owen's life—sounded terrible to her own ears, and she glossed over the specifics in her recount.

Finally, they dropped her back at Dot's house. A new van was parked at the murder scene, and the officer driving her mentioned that the pathologist had arrived from Victoria Island to examine the body. Brianna's lips thinned. It wouldn't take a genius to conclude that Owen's death was murder.

Brianna's chest was tight. She rubbed it hard, but the anguish didn't abate. Dot, her loving aunt, was now in custody for murder. The more Brianna pondered the events in her mind, the more she grew convinced that Dot was innocent and needed to be released. She could only hope that the Mounties would sort out this mess soon.

And if Dot weren't the murderer, that meant that the real killer was wandering free. If Brianna was the only one who believed in Dot, was it up to her to prove her aunt's innocence?

Let the cops do their job, a nasty voice of reason that sounded suspiciously like Greg whispered in her mind. *Don't worry your pretty little head about it. Leave the investigations to the professionals.*

Brianna bit her lip. Maybe the voice was right. What did she know about solving a crime? She was only a former business consultant and a future café owner. She had no qualifications that would help. And what if she made things worse with her meddling?

Brianna corralled Zola from the pasture where she'd hastily shoved the goat before leaving, to the field she'd meant to bring her ages ago, in the time she now thought of as P.C., or pre-confession. Once Zola was safely ensconced in her field, contentedly munching grass, Brianna stumbled to her bike. She hoped the bike ride would clear her terrible fog of dismay, but she didn't have high hopes. Her beloved aunt was a prime murder suspect, and Brianna didn't know what to do about it.

Brianna parked her bicycle at a bike rack in a parking lot at the far end of the harbor. Grasping her tin, she walked down a wooden ramp that led to the floating docks of Snuggler's Cove Marina. She breathed the salty air deeply and relished the cool sea breeze that filled every corner of her lungs. It didn't dispel her aching sadness and horror over her aunt's fate, but it was pleasant, nonetheless.

The dock swayed gently against its tarred pilings. Brianna peered down a crack between dock and piling and smiled at the anemones and sea stars clinging to the wooden post. Lines clinked softly in the afternoon breeze against masts, and Brianna turned down the residents' wharf.

Here, the dock was lined with float homes. The square dwellings strained against their moorings on either side of the walkway.

She adored the float home culture. Each home was painted a gloriously brilliant hue, and most had details exhibiting their owner's personality. The bright pink home on the left was festooned with glittery ribbons, the lime green and midnight blue one next to it showcased driftwood sculptures on its tiny porch, and the large log cabin-style home across the way proudly displayed whirligigs on the roof among copious potted plants.

A teenaged boy leaned over the roof patio of this last house and yelled down to Brianna, "Hey, new girl. Mom says you should check your mailbox. There's something for you in it."

Brianna stopped and held up her hand to block the sunlight. The boy grinned down at her, his impish face anchored by a wide nose and swept-back, dark brown hair.

"Thanks," she called back. "I'm Brianna, by the way."

"Nice to meet you, neighbor." He gave her a salute. "Joel. Your mailbox has an invite to the dock party next week. Fair warning, it's always full of old farts yapping about floats and fishing. But maybe that's your thing."

"Cheeky devil," she said, a grin crossing her face despite her preoccupation. "Thanks for the warning."

Joel waved and disappeared. Chuckling, Brianna continued along her way. Near the end of the dock, she stopped at her door. It was painted a brilliant blue and surrounded by cheery orange trim. The colors made Brianna's shoulders straighten with hope every time she saw them. Maybe Dot's situation wasn't as dire as it looked.

The float home was so far removed from her neutral-colored condo with its carefully understated décor, she could hardly believe she lived here, even after a whole month of occupancy. It felt right, somehow, righter than Vancouver ever had.

True to Joel's word, a note was tucked into her wooden mailbox under its hinged lid. She extracted it and unfolded the paper. The invitation welcomed Brianna to the neighborhood and asked her to join the group next Saturday for a barbecue. Smiling, Brianna slid the note into her pocket. Old farts or not, she wouldn't pass up an opportunity to meet her fellow islanders.

Brianna tucked her key in the door and pushed into her home. The faintest sway underfoot and ocean views from every window were the only indications that she was in a floating house. Inside, the compact space held every amenity that she needed. A cozy propane fireplace had been built into a corner, flanked by a floor-to-ceiling window on one side and a glass-paned sliding garage door on the other. The door led to a tiny patio, and Brianna left it open during warmer days for fresh sea breezes. Only once had a seagull investigated the living room, and Brianna had quickly shooed the creature back outside where it belonged before it discovered her dinner. The ballast it had released on her floor had taken longer to clean up.

A long window seat on the opposite wall ended in a narrow built-in bookshelf, and Brianna had spent more than one lazy hour lounging in the sun with a favorite novel. She looked forward to stormy weather, when she could accompany her reading with a mug of hot chocolate as wind whipped the sea into a froth outside her window. Next to the reading nook, a compact kitchen was tucked into the corner. It was nothing compared to her industrial kitchen at the Golden Moon, but it worked well for preparing dinner.

Stairs leading to a ladder climbed up to the loft, where her bed lay under a wide skylight. Dot had given her a coverlet from her travels colored a brilliant turquoise and embroidered with tiny pieces of mirror. It wasn't anything Brianna would have thought to choose herself, but she smiled every time the mirrors dazzled in the sun streaming through the skylight.

She'd been collecting items for decoration ever since she'd moved in. They weren't nearly as eclectic as her aunt's choices, but they were far more debonair than Brianna was used to. She'd gone with a nautical theme in honor of the ocean around her, and framed charts and an old ship's wheel adorned her walls. She'd even found a huge decorative sailor's knot in thick jute rope that hung in pride of place in a window.

She'd only considered the float home when her aunt Dot—as free-spirited and quirky as ever—had pushed the advertisement her way. Once Brianna had laid eyes on pictures of the little home, something about the compactness, the bright colors, and the cluster of other float homes around it had drawn her in like a toddler to candy. She wanted desperately to live there, and it was an easy choice to spend the rest of her husband's life insurance payout on the place.

Brianna set her tin of baked goods on the table and sighed in happiness. Then her mood turned wistful. As fraught as her and Greg's relationship had been at the end—his death had sorrow, relief, and guilt at her relief all churned together in a mess of emotions—she still hadn't fully grown used to a solitary life. Part of her reveled in the freedom, especially when she spied her overstuffed couch that Greg would have ordered out of the house on sight, or the knickknacks she'd found at a flea market and had lined up on the top of the windowsill. But another part of her whispered at the too-quiet home and the lack of companionship.

She shook her head to rid it of the unwelcome doubts. This was her chance to reinvent herself, to find out who she really was without Greg. It was a frightening notion. Did she want to know? What if she looked, and nothing greeted her questing eyes but a scared mouse who never knew what she was doing?

If only Dot were here to keep her company.

A knock on the door interrupted her reverie, and

Brianna jumped to answer it, relieved at the distraction.

Chapter 7

On the dock before her door stood an older man with a bristly gray beard and half-moon glasses. He wore a plaid flannel shirt and an expectant look.

"Hello," Brianna said in a pleasant tone. Was this man a new neighbor? She hadn't met many of them yet, but what better way to get involved with her new community than to socialize with her fellow float home owners?

"I'm here to introduce myself," he said in a gruff tone. "Magnus Pickleton, owner of the marina. Mind if I come in?"

Without waiting for Brianna's invitation, Magnus pushed past her into the house. Bemused, Brianna closed the door behind him and stared at her visitor.

"It's nice to meet you, Magnus. I'm Brianna West."

"I hear you're opening up some sort of cheese café." Magnus gazed around the float home with critical eyes. "You might say I'm something of an expert in the subject of cheese."

"Oh, are you a fan of cheese?" She could overlook his awkward gruffness if she'd already found an avid customer.

Magnus drew himself up to his full height—a hair taller than Brianna's average stature—and looked down at her. A crumb of whatever he'd had for breakfast waggled in his beard.

"A fan?" he said as if the word were the greatest insult.

His already wrinkled forehead furrowed into deep trenches of displeasure. "A fan. As if cheese were the latest pop singer. No, I am a serious connoisseur of the great art of cheesemaking, an ardent friend of fromagerie, a humble student of fermented dairy."

Brianna bit her lips to avoid chuckling. Magnus didn't strike her as having a humble bone in his body.

"I'm glad to hear it," she said in a pleasant tone, choosing to ignore Magnus's affronted stare. "You'll feel right at home in the Golden Moon when it opens. If there's one thing I know, it's how to cook with cheese. My family has a tradition of cheese, in fact. My grandmother grew up on a dairy—"

"I admit, I'm highly skeptical of all this cooking with cheese you plan to do," Magnus interrupted again. Brianna didn't sigh out loud, but it was a near thing. "Marring the purity of a good cheese is risky business."

"You'll have to decide for yourself when I open the café." Brianna moved toward the door to give the older man a hint. She'd had enough of his critical barbs and creased brow. "It was lovely meeting you."

"Wait, I have an invitation for you." He forced the words from tight lips as if pulling apart cold toffee. "The Gourmand Society has voted that you may attend our next meeting. As president, I expressed my misgivings at this generous offer, but I was overruled. However, I do agree that your use of cheese should be monitored, and this is exactly our jurisdiction."

Brianna blinked at him. If that was an invitation, she'd almost missed it beneath the insults.

"The Gourmand Society? What is your jurisdiction?"

Brianna hadn't heard anything about a special society on the island. Was there a governing body for the dairy industry in Snuggler's Cove? She wouldn't put it past town council to institute something of the sort. From her minor dealings with the council so far, it seemed overly enthusiastic in its pursuit of making the island the very best it could be.

"Maybe govern isn't the correct word," Magnus allowed. "But we very closely watch the cheese scene on Driftwood Island and on all the surrounding Gulf Islands. We take our role very seriously."

"You mean to say you're a cheese club," Brianna said, unable to suppress her grin.

Magnus glared at her but didn't deign to acknowledge her slight.

"We carefully monitor the cheese industry, yes. Driftwood and the surrounding islands have a long and proud tradition of cheese-making. Why, the island even has a herd of water buffalo to produce mozzarella the way the Italians intended. It's truly a remarkable scene. One which we do not want muddied with substandard products."

Brianna felt a retort rise to her lips, but a wet towel of doubt smothered the heat of her anger. Was she playing with something that was too big for her? Maybe she didn't belong here, sticking her toes into the curds and whey of established island life. Did a desire to start afresh and a love of cheese give her the right to barge in?

She squared her shoulders. It was only cheese, for pity's sake. Magnus and his minions didn't own the island, as far as she was aware. She had every right to cook a blue cheese Danish pastry if she wanted to and sell it to others if they wanted to buy. Time and profits would prove her belonging and worth, not some jumped-up old man with a dictatorial gleam in his eye.

"I would love to attend the next meeting of the Gourmand Society," she said sweetly. If Magnus didn't want her there, well, that only made her more determined to come. "I would be happy to introduce myself and bring a sampling of treats for everyone to enjoy."

Magnus eyed her, but she didn't give away her annoyance in her expression of bland pleasantness.

"Humph. Well, then. The next meeting is on Wednesday evening at the community hall, six o'clock."

On a whim, Brianna swooped over to her baking tin, cracked open the metal lid, and presented it to Magnus.

"Please help yourself to a scone," she said. "Freshly baked this morning. Asiago, apricot, and jalapeño."

Magnus visibly recoiled at the list of ingredients, but he gingerly reached out a large, blunt-fingered hand to grab the topmost scone.

"Thanks," he said, eyeing the scone as if it might bite him. He turned and wandered out the door.

"See you on Wednesday," Brianna called after him in a bright voice, then she shut the door and leaned against it. Her stomach heaved with silent laughter at the absurdity of Magnus. Was this how island life operated? She had a lot to learn if so, although she'd held her own against the grumpy old man.

Once she was alone, Brianna's thoughts drifted back to Dot. She amused herself by imagining how Dot would have reacted to Magnus—with gentle teasing, no doubt—then her jaw tightened. Why was she content to let the Mounties deal with this situation? They had a confession. Why would they delve any deeper?

Brianna was the only one who believed in her aunt's innocence. Dot was clearly covering up for someone, and Brianna needed to figure out what was going on if she wanted to save Dot. Her aunt might be content to take the fall for this death, but Brianna couldn't rest until she found the real murderer and her aunt was cleared of all charges.

Leave it to the professionals, Greg's phantom voice whispered to her. *Your uneducated meddling will only make things worse.*

She straightened her spine and wrinkled her nose at the words. She wasn't entirely clueless. Greg had brought his work home with him often enough and pontificated to her about his cases. She'd picked up plenty of techniques along the way, even if he had repressed any involvement on her part. She had the guts to continue her café despite Magnus Pickleton's insults. Why should she lie down like a doormat when her aunt's freedom was at stake? If she didn't do anything, Dot was as good as gone. It was up to Brianna to free Dot, and she wouldn't back down, no matter who stood in her way.

Brianna picked up her purse and marched to the door. If she'd learned anything from Greg, it was the importance of a good team to a successful investigation. She needed backup.

Brianna pulled into the driveway of Happy Hearts preschool twenty minutes later, damp with exertion and grim-faced with resolve. She leaned her bike against a brick wall and gazed up at a cheery mural of waving sunflowers, butterflies, and bright-eyed squirrels that was painted above the door. Children's voices chattered from an open window around the corner. Brianna took a deep breath to calm her overactive heart.

By the time Macy wandered out of the building ten minutes later, Brianna had cooled enough to greet her with some composure.

"My break is short," Macy said, "but I'm glad to see you. What's up?"

"I found my aunt Dot's neighbor Owen Montague dead with Dot's pitchfork stabbed in his back," Brianna said without preamble. "Dot confessed to the murder, and now she's in custody."

Macy's face drained of color, and she put her hand against the brick wall of the preschool entryway without looking at it. She stared at Brianna with wide eyes.

"Why would Dot do something like that?" she whispered. "I can't imagine her ever murdering someone. She cries when Stacey Nazarian's pigs drive by on their way to the abattoir."

"I don't believe she did it."

Macy gave her a sympathetic look. "I know that's what you want to believe, but if Dot confessed…" A gleam of hope sparkled in her eyes. "What makes you say that?"

"Exactly what you said. Dot being a murderer is so out of character as to be hardly worthy of mentioning. But I do think she's hiding something. She confessed for a reason, and I need to figure out why. Who is she protecting?" Brianna rubbed her cheeks with her hands and took a deep breath. "If I'm right, there's a killer on the loose, and an innocent woman is locked up for a crime she didn't commit. I need to figure this out."

Macy was nodding before Brianna finished speaking. She pushed away from her support wall and stood straight.

"*We* need to figure this out." Macy shivered. "I don't like the idea of a murderer wandering the streets of Snuggler's Cove unchecked. And if your aunt is innocent, we can't let her take the fall."

"Thanks, Macy." Brianna's eyes grew warm. She hadn't known whether she could count on her old friend to believe her or support her. That she could rely on Macy meant a lot to Brianna. She didn't think many of her Vancouver acquaintances would have accepted her mission with the same unflinching trust.

Macy placed her hand on Brianna's shoulder with a gentle squeeze. "Just remember to keep an open mind as we search. There is still a small chance that Dot is the culprit. I don't want you to be blinded just because she's your aunt."

Brianna nodded, even as her stomach twisted at the thought that Dot might be responsible. "I will, I promise."

"Good." Macy let her go and clapped her hands. "So, what's the plan?"

"Dot said something as she was being taken away." Brianna frowned as Dot's words floated back to her out of the fog of that terrible moment. "'It's always the people closest to the victim.' She was trying to say that she was a likely suspect, but we can take her words another way. Aren't most murders done by someone close to the victim? And not geographically close, relationship-wise close. What about Owen's wife, Tansy, and their son?"

"Jay?" Macy raised her eyebrow. "If he's a murderer, then I hate vanilla flavoring in my coffee."

"He seemed genuinely shocked," Brianna admitted. "If he were acting, he's very good at it. Tansy was over the top, in my opinion, but everyone's different when it comes to grief. I stared at the wall for hours that first day when I found out about Greg. Some wailing and gnashing of teeth feels justified."

"It's worth checking out," Macy said. "Give them today to cool off and absorb what happened, then take them some of your baking tomorrow. No one can resist that for long, no matter how surly. Sniff around for clues."

Brianna nodded and squared her shoulders. Her first interview in her investigation. A part of her wriggled with excitement even through her grim resolve and self-doubt. She didn't expect much from the upcoming conversation, but she'd be doing *something* to help Dot, and that made it a worthwhile endeavor.

"I hope you're right." She threw her leg over her

bicycle and gave Macy a parting smile. "The last time we spoke, Tansy was sobbing and yelling at me. It will take a cheesy miracle to get past that."

Chapter 8

Brianna tried to concentrate on café paperwork for the rest of the afternoon, but it was difficult with thoughts of Dot swirling in her mind. When she finally gave up and went to bed, sleep was a long time coming.

The next morning, Brianna woke early and threw herself into test-baking. By the time her carpenter arrived in the café's dining room, Brianna was wheeling down the alley and away from the café. When her bike crested the hill leading to Dot's house, the bucolic scene didn't comfort her like it had done the day before. Among the fluffy sheep and rolling fields hid a killer, and her aunt was caught in the crossfire. Clouds skittered across the sun and darkened patches of grass with chasing shadows. Despite the warmth of the summer's day and her exertion, Brianna shivered.

She wheeled into Dot's gravel driveway again and dropped her bike against the railing, then darted into the house and rustled in Dot's kitchen for a paper plate. She finally uncovered a stack patterned in vibrant swirls of color in a bottom drawer. They weren't exactly mourning hues, but Brianna took what she could get. She didn't trust that she and Tansy would be pals enough for Tansy to return her tin.

She transferred a fresh batch of scones to the plate and carefully walked out the door. She took the driveway this time despite the distance. She didn't want to be accused of sneaking in, not with the barn being a crime scene and her aunt the culprit. Besides, Brianna didn't trust herself not to drop the treats while climbing over the fence.

Zola watched her crunch down the driveway, and Brianna waved. She knew it was silly to wave to a goat, but she felt badly for the animal. It wasn't Zola's fault that Dot had left her alone. Brianna promised herself to come every day to check on the goat.

"Until Dot is back," Brianna told herself fiercely. She was coming back. Brianna would do everything she could to make that happen.

The Montague's driveway stretched like melted mozzarella as Brianna trudged forward, both eager to question mother and son and dreading the confrontation. She didn't expect a warm welcome from either of them, but she had to at least try to speak with the two. If they weren't suspects, they still might know something. Either way, she needed to do this.

On the porch of the Montague's white-sided farmhouse, Brianna lifted her fist and knocked. After a long moment, Jay flung open the door.

"Oh look, it's the bearer of bad news," he said, his face twisted in a sneer that looked out of place on a face that tended toward mild-mannered. "Come to tell us that someone else is dead?"

Brianna bit her lip but held her ground. She thrust forward the plate. "I came to offer my condolences. You just suffered a tragedy, and I can't help feeling a connection, seeing as I was the one who found your father."

"And your aunt is the murderer," Jay spat out.

"I never thought she could do something like this," Brianna said truthfully. "It's such a shock to me, too."

Jay opened his mouth to retort, but his mother's voice drifted from another room.

"Let her in, Jay. She's not to blame for all this."

Jay scowled but stepped aside for Brianna to enter. She skirted the angry young man and followed the voice through a wide hallway with polished wooden floors and expensive-looking paintings on the walls. Brianna glanced into the living room as she passed, and her eyebrows rose. Everything in the room screamed quality and expense, from claw-footed couches to the immaculate wool carpet, a far cry from Dot's well-worn Persian rug. The water buffalo business must have been booming.

Tansy sat at a rustic yet clearly expensive kitchen table made of an unfinished slab of wood. The kitchen was in a farmhouse style, with white cupboards and old-fashioned handles, but everything was new and gleaming. It wasn't only a showpiece, though, as evidenced by the bloody cutting boards and knives on the granite counter. Tansy must not have finished cleaning up from her truncated chore of chicken butchering yesterday.

Tansy nursed a large mug of tea at the table. Her blue eyes were dry, but she looked tired. "Brianna, wasn't it?" Tansy waved at the chair across from her. "Have a seat. Jay, fetch Brianna a mug, will you?"

Jay glowered but did as his mother bid him. He dropped a floral-patterned mug in front of Brianna then leaned against the counter to stare at their guest. Brianna shifted in her seat, uneasy at being the center of his attention.

"The pigs need feeding," Tansy said pointedly at Jay. "Go on. I'll save you a scone for later."

Jay folded his arms in protest, but after a glare from his mother, he huffed and left without another word. A moment later, Brianna saw him cross the yard beyond the kitchen window with a pail of slops in his hand.

"He's a good boy," Tansy said, gazing at her son through the glass. "He didn't deserve all this."

Tansy covered her eyes and took a shaky breath.

"I'm so sorry for your loss," Brianna said gently. She pushed the treats toward Tansy and poured herself some tea, allowing Tansy to dab at her eyes with a tissue and collect herself.

"It was kind of you to bring us these." Tansy waved at the scones and picked one up. She bit into it, and her eyelids fluttered when flavors hit her tongue. "Oh, my. This is delicious. I'll have to visit your café when you open. Will you do smoothies?"

"I hadn't thought about them," Brianna said. "But I'm always open to customer suggestions." She turned the hot mug around in her hands, not wanting to break the relative calm that she and Tansy had established but needing answers for Dot. "May I ask you a few questions?"

Tansy's eyes darted to hers and her brow contracted. "What kind of questions?" she asked.

"It's just—" Brianna tried to choose her words carefully. "I find it very hard to believe that Dot—did what it looks like she did." She didn't want to mention the word "murder" to Owen's grieving widow.

Tansy's eyes widened. "What are you saying? You think the woman who confessed over the body didn't do it? What kind of nonsense is this?" She half-stood from the table and leaned over it with her hands on the top. "What, you think someone else killed my husband? Are you here to accuse me?" She gasped loudly. "You are. I would never kill Owen. How could you even think that?"

"No, no." Brianna shook her head vigorously. That had been exactly what she'd been thinking, but she needed to diffuse the situation before it got out of hand and Jay came back to throw her bodily out of the house. "That's not it at all. I only wanted to get your opinion on whether anyone else might have a grudge against Owen. It feels to me like Dot was covering up for someone else."

Tansy sat heavily, breathing like a wounded rhinoceros. She stared at Brianna for a while. Brianna waited with her breath held.

"Jay and I were butchering and processing chickens from sunrise to when you found us," Tansy said finally. "We hardly had a moment to ourselves all morning. Owen had gone to check on the water buffalo—we rent a field with a pond on the west side of the island—then he was supposed to come back and finish his farm chores. I hadn't seen him since he'd left our bed that morning." Tansy's eyes filled with tears, and she dashed them away.

"I understand that Dot is the most likely suspect, given that she confessed," Brianna said. "Since she's locked up now, my poking around will only matter if she's innocent, so you have nothing to lose by helping me, and you stand to gain finding the real killer, if it isn't Dot." Brianna gripped her mug in both hands and locked eyes with Tansy. "Was there anyone else who might have a motive for killing Owen?"

Tansy's eyes flickered, then she stared into Brianna's.

"Owen was having an affair," she whispered. Her eyes filled with tears again, but this time, she didn't brush them away. They dripped onto the tabletop and left tiny puddles next to Tansy's untouched mug of tea. "With Diana Bartley. He told me a few days ago, but he promised that they were over and that he wanted to fix things with me, go to marriage counseling, whatever it took to make things right." She heaved a sob. "Of course I said yes. He's my husband—was my husband—and he made a mistake. Forgiveness is a crucial ingredient in a good marriage."

Privately, Brianna considered that her own tendency to forgive Greg could have been tempered with more assertiveness, but she didn't know the dynamic between Tansy and Owen. Tansy didn't look like a pushover, and maybe Owen had been sincere in his apologies. In any event, Tansy's confession gave her a potential lead.

"Wait, I recognize that name. Is Diana a relation to Shaun Bartley?" That was the name of Brianna's carpenter, who was currently working on her café.

Tansy snorted. "You could say so. They're married, after all. I wouldn't doubt if Shaun had found out. He's a loose cannon, that one. Flying off the handle wouldn't surprise me at all, and someone messing with his wife?" She gave an exaggerated shiver. "All I'm saying is that if your aunt hadn't confessed, I would be pointing my finger in his direction."

"I see." Brianna sipped her tea then pushed back her chair. "Thank you so much for confiding in me."

"Be careful," Tansy said with worry creasing her brow. "Don't let Shaun know what you're about. I wouldn't want to see you get caught in the middle of all this. Maybe you should go to the police."

"I have no evidence except my belief that Dot is innocent." Brianna shrugged, feeling the weight of her task on her shoulders. "No, I need to give them more than that. If I can come up with something tangible, I will certainly let the authorities know."

Tansy nodded, her eyes never leaving Brianna's face. "Good. You take care of yourself, now."

Brianna walked back to her bicycle, her mind whirling. Maybe when Macy got off work at four o'clock, she could help Brianna interrogate Shaun. Macy had a way of drawing people out by using her natural outpouring of empathy that made others confide in her. Brianna wasn't bad, although she relied more on her baking to win her friends, but Macy was a master.

In the meantime, Brianna had an appointment with a food photographer, who was due to take photos of a few baked goods and cheeses for her menu and website. Brianna's eye caught on the small white goat in the pasture. Zola's head poked through the fence, and she stared at Brianna with a focused gaze. She wasn't even chewing alfalfa.

"Are you lonely?" Brianna wandered over to the goat and reached down to scratch Zola's head. The goat pushed against her hand with enjoyment, and Brianna's heart squeezed. How could she give the little goat more attention? She was used to Dot hanging out in the pasture with her every day.

Brianna looked around for inspiration, and her gaze fixed on the ripped old bike trailer beside the porch. She glanced at Zola appraisingly.

"Want to go on a little adventure?" she asked. Zola butted her hand, and Brianna took that as a yes. It took a few minutes of cursing and searching for tools, but she managed to affix the trailer to her bicycle. Once she tied a rope around Zola's halter, she opened the gate. The goat trotted beside her and hopped into the trailer like she'd done it many times before. Brianna narrowed her eyes at the animal.

"Dot takes you around sometimes, doesn't she? You're a lucky goat, you are."

Brianna threw a bundle of alfalfa in a side pocket of the trailer, zipped the flap of the main compartment closed, and swung her leg over her saddle. Zola's weight pulled on her bicycle, and Brianna changed gears with a grimace. She'd be getting her workout today, that was for sure. Hopefully, she could make it up the hills in time for her appointment with the photographer.

Chapter 9

Brianna was breathless and red-faced when she pulled into the alley beside her café. Hammering noises floated out of the propped-open door where her carpenter Shaun was hard at work. She didn't want to disturb him—partly because she didn't want to interrupt his work, but mostly because he might be a murderer—so she quietly unlocked the side door that led directly to the kitchen.

Zola bleated, and Brianna hurried to unzip the trailer. She snatched the rope dangling from Zola's halter as it whisked by during Zola's escape attempt.

"Not so fast, you crazy critter," she muttered. "Stay here and enjoy the alley while I deal with my cheese."

Brianna tied Zola's rope to a pipe on the side of the building. While Zola poked her nose at a clump of dandelions sprouting from the weedy gravel, Brianna entered the kitchen on quiet footsteps. Oldies radio was pumping from the front dining room, and Brianna's shoulders relaxed. Shaun would never know she was here.

She bustled around, plating different cheeses on platters and cutting boards, pulling out her fanciest cheese knives, and arranging scones and pastries that she'd baked early that morning. When the clock on her phone indicated her appointment time, she exited via the alley, gave Zola a pat and a handful of alfalfa, and strode to the front to wait for the photographer.

She didn't wait long. A short man her age with glasses and a bulky camera bag swinging from his polo-shirted shoulder hailed her.

"Brianna West?" he cried. "Frederick Baxter. I'm here to take pictures of your cheese."

Brianna smiled and shook his hand in a firm handshake. "Please, come this way. I don't want to disturb my carpenter."

Something wasn't right in the alley, but Brianna couldn't put her finger on it. Was something missing? Her bike was there.

"What sort of pictures are you looking for today?" Frederick asked, pushing Brianna's unease out of her mind.

"Just pictures of the baked goods and cheeses. The dining room isn't ready yet. The images will go on my website and promotional materials."

Brianna gestured at Frederick to enter the kitchen through the already open door. Frederick paused in the doorway.

"I'm not sure that's entirely food safe," he said.

Brianna poked her head over his shoulder and gasped. A small white goat stood on her beautiful butcher block counter with her nose in a plate of Havarti. The contents of the scone plate were already decimated. Zola looked up at their entrance and chewed with a satisfied stare.

"Zola!" Brianna cried.

She pushed past Frederick and leaped to the goat's side. With trembling arms, she grasped the goat around the middle and hauled her bodily off the counter.

Frederick jumped aside as Brianna barreled through the door into the alley and dropped the goat into the trailer.

Zola bleated and pushed against Brianna's hand. Was that her apology? Brianna sighed out her frustrations and scratched the goat's head. Zola couldn't help her nature. She was a curious, hungry animal.

"I guess you like my baking," Brianna murmured. "Thank you for the compliment. But let's stick to hay for now, shall we?"

She shoved a handful of alfalfa into the trailer and zipped the screen closed. Zola bent her head dutifully to the hay and started to munch. With a sigh, Brianna turned back to the carnage in the kitchen.

"Do you have any more product?" Frederick examined the plates of food. "Look, this cutting board hasn't been touched yet. The good news is that it only has to look tasty, and no one will know if there's goat hair in the pictures."

Brianna shuddered. "I'll have to bleach everything down thoroughly after this. Sorry about that. Maybe start with the cutting board and I'll plate up some fresh food."

Once the photographer pronounced himself satisfied, Brianna waved him out of the kitchen and released Zola from her trailer.

"You be good," she warned the goat as she tied the animal up to the pipe with a stronger knot. "I'm going to clean up your mess, then we'll go for a walk."

Zola watched her from the doorway as Brianna scrubbed the counters and disposed of contaminated food. Once everything was cleaned to her satisfaction, she closed the door behind her and untied Zola's rope. The two of them strode toward the road in the warm spring afternoon.

Brianna felt ridiculous walking a goat through town, but it was a sign of the island's laidback attitude that no one looked at her askance. Many people greeted her cheerily, and one or two petted Zola. Brianna tried to imagine walking a goat in downtown Vancouver, and she snorted with laughter.

Zola enjoyed munching on grass on the boulevard beside the ocean walkway. When she relieved herself, Brianna found a baggie and dealt with the mess like a dog owner would. She shook her head at the direction her life had taken her. What would Greg have said if he could see her now? He'd always been vehemently opposed to pets, and here she was, looking after a goat of all creatures. Brianna lifted her chin and smiled at the next passerby.

Back at the café with Zola safely tied to the pipe once more, Brianna loitered in the alley with the animal. She listened to the oldies radio that pumped out of the café's open window until Macy's red hatchback bumped into the alley. Macy popped out of the driver's side and strode toward her. A splatter of pink paint decorated the sleeve of her blouse.

"I'm here." Macy cracked her knuckles and put her hands on her hips. "What did you find out from Tansy this morning? What's our plan of attack?"

"Diana Bartley and Owen Montague were having an affair," Brianna said in a hushed voice. She didn't want pedestrians walking by to hear her news, nor did she want her neighbor Annalise in the yarn shop to overhear. To her consternation, Macy let out a horrified gasp then a cackle of laughter.

"Are you kidding? Diana likes to set herself up as the paragon of virtue, and her marriage to Shaun as the epitome of wedded bliss. Do you know how many times she's looked down her nose at me for having Oaklyn without getting hitched? Oh, the irony."

"Keep your voice down," Brianna hissed. "Shaun's in my café right now, and he's a murder suspect."

Macy sobered. "I can see that. He threw his plate across the room at a restaurant once because his fries weren't hot. If anyone were capable of a crime of passion, it would be him."

Brianna grew cold. Was she really considering confronting Shaun? If he were the murderer, what would stop him killing again so she couldn't tell others the truth? Was she in serious danger from the carpenter?

She gritted her teeth. She had to do this for Dot. The police wouldn't do anything based on her hunches, not when they had a confession sitting in lock-up. She needed more evidence to present to them.

"We won't confront him with anything," she said at last. "That would be too dangerous. But let's see if we can pry any interesting information out of him, like whether he knew if Diana was having an affair."

"That's not going to be easy," Macy warned, but she

rubbed her hands together with a gleam in her eyes. "But I'm ready."

Chapter 10

Brianna took a deep breath and entered the side door that led to her kitchen. She and Macy peeked through the door of the café. Shaun whistled while he measured a board, the tawny bristle on his large head glinting in the window's bright light. Was he happy because he was oblivious to the drama unfolding on Driftwood Island, or because he had murdered his romantic rival?

"Do you have anything to feed him?" Macy whispered. "Best way to butter someone up is with lots of butter."

A chuckle escaped Brianna's mouth, and she turned to the counter where a few extra scones untouched by Zola waited in a container. She found a plate, tossed a few of the baked goods on it, then squared her shoulders.

"Ready?" she mouthed to Macy. When her friend nodded, Brianna lifted her chin and marched into the café like she was walking into battle, with Macy flanking her.

Shaun glanced up and frowned at the interruption until his eyes lit on the plate. His fingers let go of the end of the measuring tape and it snapped into place.

"Hi, Shaun," Brianna said brightly. "I thought you could use a snack after all your hard work."

"Thanks, Brianna. Hi, Macy." Shaun rose to his full height and grabbed a scone from the plate. He leaned against a wall and bit into the scone with delight. "I tell you, working for a café was the smartest job I've ever picked up."

"Glad to hear you like the baking," Brianna said.

"Don't be fooled by her modesty," Macy said in a mock-whisper. "She hands out scones for the ego-boost."

Shaun chuckled. "Happy to oblige if the snacks keep coming."

"I miss having your son in my class," Macy said. "Such a scamp, but was there anyone with a cuter smile than little Jack?"

Shaun grinned. "Not many, I think. He's doing well at elementary school now. Giving the teachers a run for their money, from what I hear. Takes after his father." Shaun beamed with paternal pride.

"How's Diana these days?" Macy asked casually. "I haven't seen her for a while. I used to have nice chats with her at pick-up time."

A grimace dashed across Shaun's face like the fleeting clouds that had dimmed the fields this afternoon. It was gone almost before Brianna registered the emotion.

"Good, good," Shaun said with a shrug. "Lots of work at the salon, you know how it is. And Jack keeps her busy."

"I'll have to stop in sometime," Macy said. "I could use a haircut. She seemed a little down the last time I passed the salon, that's why I was wondering. If there's any trouble, or anything I can do, just let me know. I'm happy to help."

Shaun's jaw tightened. "She's fine. And we're fine. Better than fine, in fact. And if there was anything wrong,

I would move mountains to make things right."

Macy glanced at Brianna, who held her breath. That was evidence enough to pry a little deeper.

"I'm glad to hear you're well," Brianna said. "And if I can make your life a little better with scones, you know I will." She beamed at her carpenter and ran her hand over the half-built counter. "I'm loving your work so far. It's too bad you can't work all night too."

Shaun laughed, the tenseness of earlier forgotten. "I do work a lot, just not always here. Two nights ago, I was fixing up the marina's broken step for Magnus. I stayed until late trying to finish up. He's a stickler for the details, Magnus is. If I hadn't stuck around, he'd be on me the next morning like a fruit fly on a banana. I would have slept in until noon the next morning, if Diana had let me."

Brianna's lips thinned, and she exchanged another glance with Macy, although this time their looks were less hopeful. Shaun's interaction with his wife Diana didn't exclude him from being a suspect in Owen's death—he could have rushed over to the Montagues between leaving his house and going to work, with Diana none the wiser—but it certainly didn't help prove he was the murderer. Brianna decided to switch tactics.

"Did you hear about the murder yesterday morning?" Brianna said.

Shaun glanced up at her with concern on his face. If he were hiding something, he was a very good liar.

"Diana mentioned it, but she didn't know the details," he said. "Strange, given that she works in the salon. They always know everything there. Do you know who died?"

"Owen Montague," Macy said quietly.

Shaun's face darkened at the sound of his rival's name, then he ducked his face downward to hide the light of wild hope in his eyes.

"That's terrible," he said after a moment collecting himself. "A man, dead. His poor wife. She must be heartbroken. Nothing cuts like the loss of a spouse." He looked up again, his face once more a mask of concern. "Do they know who did it?"

"They have someone in custody," Brianna said. "But it's not certain that they have the right person. The motives are a bit wobbly."

Shaun drained his mug and set it on the half-built counter, then grabbed his tape measure again and stretched it out.

"I don't want to speak ill of the dead," he said casually. "But Owen was a little too influential with the ladies, if you know what I mean. I overheard old Hilda Button in the hardware store last week whispering about him and Esmerelda Alonso meeting in secret." He shrugged and jotted down a number on the wood with a pencil. "Who knows? Maybe he ticked her off."

Macy widened her eyes at Brianna. Brianna eyed Shaun, but he was studiously averting his eyes from her gaze. Brianna couldn't help suspect that Shaun was trying to deflect her scrutiny, but was that because he was the killer, or because he wanted the heat off him and Diana? Reading between the lines, Shaun knew about his wife's involvement with the dead man. If she'd learned anything from Greg's brought-home work, it was that money and love were the two most powerful motivators for murder, and jealousy in the hot-tempered Shaun was too strong to ignore. In Brianna's books, that made the carpenter someone to watch.

However, that didn't mean she should ignore Shaun's lead about this Esmerelda Alonso. It just meant that Brianna wouldn't stay in the café alone with Shaun until she found out his status one way or another.

"The secrets small islands can hold, hey?" she said lightly. "I'm sure the police will figure it out soon."

Macy helped her clear away the tea things in silence. When they exited the café's kitchen through the side door into the alley, Macy pushed the door shut and leaned against it. Zola stared at her with yellow eyes.

"We cannot rule Shaun out," she said, panting. "Whew! Did you see his glee at the news of Owen's death?"

"Not surprising, given his wife was sleeping with Owen." Brianna pulled the elastic out of her hair and fluffed the tight curls while she thought. Zola grabbed her shorts with her teeth and Brianna gently pushed her away. "Not conclusive that he's the killer, but, I agree, we're not ruling him out yet. What do you know about this Esmerelda Alonso character?"

Macy's mouth twitched. "She's a character, all right. Waltzes around the town like she owns it, but not in an unfriendly way. More like she's the town's patron and we are her adoring benefactors." Macy snorted. "She writes articles for hoity-toity foodie magazines, and she doesn't let anyone forget how valued she is in the North American cuisine scene. I have no idea what's true or not. I don't read anything she writes in, and my idea of gourmet is a burger at the Stumbling Goose."

Brianna laughed. "Then let's have a gourmet pub night out, you and me. Does tomorrow work for you? My treat."

Macy's face flushed with pleasure. She checked her watch.

"Tomorrow sounds amazing. Oaklyn will be happy to have the house to herself, no doubt. But right now, I have to get home and make dinner." Macy wrapped her arms around Brianna in a swift embrace then gripped her shoulders tightly in her hands. "Don't stay in the café with Shaun alone, do you hear? There's no need to take risks like that, not until we know more."

Brianna nodded. "Good advice. I might pop into the police station after I drop off Zola, tell them about the affair in case they don't know yet. I want to check on Dot, too, see what's happening with her. Usually, they can only hold a suspect for twenty-four hours unless they ask a judge for longer. But since she confessed, I don't know what will happen. Then I have my first meeting of the Gourmand Society tonight."

"Oh my, already moving in exalted circles." Macy raised her eyebrow but spoiled the impressed expression when she giggled. "Sorry, I couldn't keep a straight face. I've only heard about that group, but—well, you'll see when you get there."

With that enigmatic statement, Macy waved goodbye and trotted to her red hatchback. Brianna loaded Zola into the trailer, slung a leg over her bike seat, and pedaled slowly after Macy with her mind churning. Shaun's clear joy at Owen's death rang all sorts of alarm bells in

Brianna's head, but she couldn't shake the feeling that something else was going on, something she hadn't uncovered yet. Shaun's lack of knowledge about the murder had felt genuine, and Brianna usually had an uncanny knack for sensing lies. But everyone could be wrong sometimes.

She pumped her legs on the pedals, back up the hill for the second time today. Her legs were growing tired, especially with Zola behind her, but Brianna pushed harder, enjoying the effort. At this rate, she'd be able to eat as much of her own baking as she wanted. Outdoor cycling was miles away from her spin class in the city, and she reveled in the warm spring air pouring into her lungs and the breeze cooling her damp skin.

She'd meant what she'd said about approaching the police station. Greg's whispers were never far from her mind, and they clearly stated that she should leave investigating to the professionals. While she wasn't in full agreement, she certainly didn't want to withhold information from them, especially if it could help exonerate Dot. Brianna assumed that they weren't even trying to investigate, not with Dot's signed confession. They might have other, more official channels to pursue in their search, and Brianna owed it to her aunt to do everything she could to uncover the truth.

Brianna crunched down the gravel driveway once again, this time leaning her bike against the pasture fence. She unzipped the trailer and led Zola back to her field, then grabbed an armful of alfalfa from the barn and tossed it over the fence. The goat trotted over when she spotted Brianna's present.

"There you go, you yellow-eyed eating machine." She scratched the white goat's head while the animal tore into the pile of alfalfa. "I'll be back tomorrow. I promise I won't let you go hungry while Dot's gone."

Brianna's eyes wandered past the barn and to the Montague's property while her fingers continued to rub Zola's head. A piece of yellow police tape fluttered in the breeze at the neighbor's barn door. Brianna stood straight. They hadn't finished processing the murder scene. Maybe the Mounties hadn't taken away all the evidence. If they considered the case cut and dry with Dot in custody, would they be looking for clues pointing to a different killer?

Brianna hung motionless for a moment, then her feet took her forward almost without conscious thought. She owed it to Dot to peek into that barn for clues before the Mounties cleaned up and any evidence was lost.

Brianna heaved herself over the fence after a careful look at the house. Since both the pickup and sedan were missing from the driveway, she was confident that the remaining Montagues were both out and wouldn't notice her trespassing. She knew it looked bad, since it was her aunt at the station, but she needed to know if there were anything to find.

Still, she kept her footsteps quiet as she approached the barn. The sun was low in the sky by this time, even with the later sunsets at the end of May, and its orange rays blinded her until she ducked under the yellow tape and entered the dim barn.

"Hey," a deep voice called out. "What are you doing?"

Chapter 11

Brianna's heart jumped and started to gallop around in her ribcage like a hungry Zola seeing a bale of alfalfa. She whirled around in the Montague's barn, her hand on her chest.

Corporal Devon Moore kneeled next to the bloodstain on the barn floor and frowned up at her. "You shouldn't be here. This is a crime scene."

After her initial shock, Brianna was relieved to see Devon. His presence here would save her a trip to the station on her bike along the dusky roads of Driftwood Island.

"I know, I'm sorry." She backed away until her legs pressed against the tape barrier. "I was next door feeding my aunt's goat, and I thought I heard noises over here. I wanted to make sure no one was tampering with the crime scene and messing up clues."

"That's not your job." Devon rubbed his forehead, clearly wondering what to do with the overzealous woman in his crime scene. "You can't be here. Wait, clues for what?"

Devon's brow contracted further, but somehow it made him even more handsome. Brianna pushed the thought away.

"I don't believe Dot Dubois killed Owen Montague." She lifted her chin in defiance. There, she'd said it. "I think she had a good reason for confessing, but that it wasn't because she stabbed him with the pitchfork."

Devon stood and ran a hand over his head. Without his work cap, his thick hair flowed freely in short, loose waves. Brianna brought her attention to his face when he spoke.

"Her case is strong," he said slowly. "I'm guarding the scene until the Victoria Island Integrated Major Crime Unit arrives to examine it. I have to tell you, it doesn't look good for your aunt. The detachment received an anonymous tip this afternoon about her whereabouts just before the murder, and it fits the narrative."

Brianna's stomach clenched with a far more unpleasant sensation than when she'd gazed at Devon's handsome face. Whoever was behind this was trying to strengthen Dot's apparent guilt.

"I really think you have the wrong person," she repeated but without any hope that her words would be heeded. "Wait, I wanted to tell you. Tansy told me today that Owen and Diana Bartley were having an affair. When I talked to Diana's husband Shaun, he clearly wasn't cut up about Owen's death, and I think he must have known about his wife's infidelity. Jealousy would be a strong motivator."

Devon's expression turned inward in thought. Then he pierced Brianna with a gaze so intense, she almost took a step backward in self-defense.

"Leave the investigation to us, Brianna West," he said sternly. Even through her tension, Brianna liked the way her name rolled off his tongue. "I promise, the detectives will figure out what really happened here."

Brianna bit her tongue against the retort she wanted

to throw back at Devon. Unfortunately, he was probably right. She should let the officers do their jobs. Maybe now that she had told Devon about the affair, he might take her aunt's confession with a grain of salt.

"When can I see my aunt?" she blurted out. "I've kept away because I know it takes time for processing and questions, but I want to see her."

"Come tomorrow morning," he said. "After nine. You'll be able to visit, then she's being transferred to a correctional center on the mainland until her trial."

Brianna's heart stuttered at the plans for Dot. Was everything finalized? She needed to find more evidence if no one else was going to.

"Okay. I'll leave you to it," she said quietly. Before she ducked under the barrier, she caught Devon's face twisted in an expression of frustration.

Brianna strode back to her bike, a fire of indignation slowly kindling in her chest. Devon was trying to put her in her place, just like Greg had done for years. Well, she was tired of that place. The whole reason for moving to Driftwood Island was to start fresh and reinvent herself. She didn't want to be pigeonholed into her safe box while the competent men ran the show. The Mounties hadn't discovered Owen and Diana's affair yet, by the look of Devon's face when she'd revealed that little nugget, so her snooping had resulted in potential evidence in the case.

Brianna mounted her bike and pushed the pedals hard with anger and determination. She wasn't going to stop looking until the truth was laid bare and Dot was free, no matter what Corporal Moore thought. Tonight, she had a date with the Gourmand Society. It sounded like just the place for a self-proclaimed foodie queen to preside over. With any luck, Esmerelda Alonso would be Brianna's next target of inquiry.

Brianna didn't have long before the start of the Gourmand Society's meeting, so she headed straight home, quickly showered, and arranged her fresh batch of blue cheese Danishes in her prettiest tin before closing the door of her float home behind her. She hoped the meeting would result in contacts within the island's food community—or maybe even an interview with a suspect—so that she could justify the time away from her paperwork and baking. The café's grand opening was looming ever closer.

The community hall was only minutes away by foot, so Brianna left her bicycle locked to the bike rack of the marina's parking lot. She wandered past shop fronts away from the water until she turned right onto a paved road that led northward. After two minutes' walking past clapboard houses and fields of sheep and vegetable gardens, the community hall appeared in a stand of trees.

The small dirt parking lot in front of a white-trimmed building was already almost filled with four vehicles. A small sign thumbtacked to a burgundy-painted pillar welcomed Brianna to the Gourmand Society meeting. Brianna took a deep breath and pulled open the door.

She entered an antechamber before another set of doors. Hooks lined one wall, and a half-open door led to a bathroom on the side. Brianna hitched her purse higher on her shoulder but had barely touched the hall's doorhandle when a figure barreled through it. Brianna had an impression of swirling scarves and a strong scent of jasmine before the figure stopped in front of her.

"You must be Brianna West," the woman said in a low, throaty voice. Long, delicate chains dangled from her ears in golden waterfalls, and her gray hair was swept back in a loose braid woven with feathers. "We were wondering if you would join us. I'm Esmerelda Alonso, but my friends call me Esme." She grabbed Brianna's hand and shook it, pulling her close for an intimate moment. "You and I will be great friends, I can tell."

She dazzled Brianna with a brilliant smile through lips painted a bright tomato red that offset the blue eyeshadow over large, hazel eyes.

"It's lovely to meet you, Esme." Brianna shook Esme's hand then gently extracted her own when it became clear that Esme wasn't letting go. "I'm pleased the Society invited me. I'm honored, especially considering I'm so new to the island and my café isn't even open yet. Driftwood seems like a welcoming place, though."

"Oh, it is, it is." Esme hitched her massive, beaded purse over her shoulder. "Except when people are being murdered. What a shocker. You heard about Owen Montague, didn't you? An entrepreneur after a gourmand's heart. The milk his water buffalos produce creates the most exquisite mozzarella, and it was his brainchild that started the enterprise." She sighed with a dramatic heave of her shoulders. "And such a fine specimen of a man, too."

Brianna was new enough to the island that most didn't know her connection to Dot. She wasn't as polished as Macy was at nosy small talk, but Dot was counting on her, so she channeled Macy's open manner and leaned closer to Esme.

"I heard other women agreed," Brianna said quietly with a glance around her to make sure no one had joined them in the entryway. "And that he didn't always deny them, if you know what I mean."

Esme's eyes flashed with recognition of Brianna's import. She leaned in conspiratorially.

"Too true," she whispered back. "You know, Owen approached me once. It was pleasant to be propositioned. Does wonders for one's ego, especially once one reaches a certain age." She laughed lightly. "Of course, I turned him down. His pretty face hid a seedy underbelly that didn't bear prodding." She shuddered. "I got too close once, and I regretted it."

"What?" Brianna's eyes widened. This was the first time she'd heard of Owen's secrets beyond his affair with Diana. She didn't have to feign curiosity when she stared at Esme. "What sort of underbelly was Owen hiding?"

"Something bad enough that he threatened me when I found out," Esme whispered, her eyes so wide they hid her blue eyeshadow. "I shouldn't say more than that. It's bad luck to speak ill of the dead." She stood straight and rearranged the scarves around her neck. "To think, I was walking the beach path that morning, immersing myself in the solitary scenery to ignite my muse, planning my latest article for Plate magazine, while Owen's life spark was being snuffed out. The tragedy of it all."

Esme glanced to the ceiling and blew a kiss upward. Brianna's lips thinned. Esme hadn't ruled herself out of the running—her alibi for the morning of the murder was weak, unless someone else had spotted her walking alone—but her motive had melted into a tiny puddle of doubt. Why would she kill Owen? Unless whatever he'd threatened her with had been frightening enough for retaliation.

Clearly, Esme felt that Dot's confession was airtight, and she was confident in exposing her secrets to the newcomer Brianna.

So, Esme wasn't ruled out, but the connection was elusive enough that Brianna didn't have anything to bring to Devon Moore to strengthen Dot's innocence.

"I heard that Dot Dubois confessed," Brianna said with a shake of her head, "but that she might not be the killer. I wonder who else it could be, though."

Esme's eyes brightened at this morsel of gossip. "Someone else? Oh, my word. Wait, you don't think—" She gasped with a hand to her mouth then leaned toward Brianna again with a whisper scented of peppermint. "I saw Owen and Susan DeVries shouting at each other in the Apple Cart parking lot last week. I didn't catch what they were saying, but I didn't think they knew each other well enough to yell, and nobody's car was dented. What do you think they were shouting about?"

With a raised eyebrow and a suggestive smile, Esme turned in a flurry of scarves to enter the bathroom.

Brianna took a moment to collect herself after her overwhelming encounter with Esmerelda Alonso. She didn't know who this Susan DeVries was, but it sounded like she was worthy of investigating. Brianna needed all the clues she could get to prove Dot's innocence.

Chapter 12

Brianna took a deep breath then entered the main hall. It was seven o'clock, and the Gourmand Society was due to convene.

"Ah, Brianna." Magnus stood up from a folding table in the center of the otherwise empty community hall. "You made it."

He didn't sound pleased about that fact, but the other faces around the table turned to stare at her with interest. Esme followed behind her and waved her ring-encrusted fingers at Brianna before she slid gracefully into a chair.

A fussy-looking man of thirty piled together a short stack of papers until they were exactly in line. He wore a checkered shirt with a bow tie neatly tied at the neck. Brianna couldn't decide if he wore it as a genuine article of clothing or to make an ironic statement. His pinched face and thick, round glasses leaned her opinion to the former.

An elderly woman with tightly permed white hair hummed softly to herself. Her fingers were busy mending a pair of purple knitted socks, but she nodded in a friendly manner toward Brianna at Magnus's words. Her sensible navy-blue cardigan had a white pansy tucked into the buttonhole.

The final person was a large, square woman wearing a long-sleeved cotton shirt that draped over her frame like a white sheet. Her close-cropped brown hair was pinned back from her serene face with bobby pins.

"We're very happy to have you, my dear," the elderly woman darning socks said in a sweet, high-pitched voice that reminded Brianna of fresh-baked cookies and warm blankets. "I'm Hilda Button, treasurer of the Gourmand Society. This is Susan DeVries, member-at-large." She nodded at the square woman, who nodded back graciously. Brianna vowed to keep an eye on the woman that Esme had named as suspect. "Quentin Flagstaff is our secretary." The fussy man gave Brianna a short, awkward wave before bowing his head with a nervous twitch and replacing his hands on his papers.

"Brianna and I are already well-acquainted," Esme purred with a mischievous smile at Brianna, which Brianna returned warily. She didn't know what Esme's game was, but she wanted to keep on the older woman's good side until she knew more.

"And I invited her." Magnus sniffed and waved Brianna impatiently to an empty chair between Susan and Esme. "Everyone is acquainted, yes, that's fine. Now, to business."

"May I introduce myself first?" Brianna spoke up. She'd already encountered Magnus's brand of overbearing before, and she didn't intend to sway with that wind. Before Magnus could say yes or no, Brianna smiled at the group. "Thank you so much for having me at your Gourmand Society meeting. My name is Brianna West, and I'll be opening the Golden Moon in under two weeks. I plan to serve all sorts of baked goods and lunch items, as long as they involve cheese of some description. I'm excited to hear more about the cheese scene on the

Gulf Islands from people as knowledgeable as yourselves."

There was no harm in buttering these folks up, especially if they had any sway in the community. Good word of mouth was vital for a café, especially in a small town. If she could get the foodie authorities talking about the Golden Moon, she'd be off to the races.

"The café isn't open yet, but I wanted to give you a sneak preview of my baking." Brianna opened the tin and passed it to Susan, who took a Danish pastry after a long look of suspicion at the baked goods. She passed the container to Hilda. "Blue cheese and pear Danishes."

"So kind," Hilda said with a pleased grin at Brianna. She passed the tin to Magnus, who glared into the depths before selecting a pastry and passing the tin to Quentin. "I'm glad you could join us tonight."

"Yes," said Esme with a pointed glance at Magnus. "Luckily, the popular vote agreed to invite you, despite opposition."

Brianna sat in her chair and fought to keep a straight face as Magnus sniffed again.

"To order, to order," he said without answering Esme's comment. "Let's start with the weekly report. Any food-related news of interest?"

"Ooo," said Hilda with excitement. Her needle never stopped moving on her socks. "Besides the Golden Moon opening soon, of course. Tia from Hilltop Farm started serving cinnamon buns as a trial at her roadside stand. They are quite scrumptious. I might even order some for my bed and breakfast next week. My guests will swoon for them, I have no doubt. Tia said she was inspired by that baking show on television, but I heard she lifted the recipe from her mother-in-law's secret cookbook that she hasn't shown anybody, ever."

"I heard her young son dropped nutmeg into the bowl by accident, and that's what gives them their edge," Esme said grandly. "But who knows the real truth. Sometimes stories are better than reality. For example, the famous chef Tom Barclay from his New York restaurant Pizzaz is rumored to meditate with his Roquefort to increase its potency. When I spoke to him last—during my latest visit to Pizzaz, Tom and I go way back, ever since I introduced him to Pierre Morel, the famed sommelier—he assured me that he does no such thing."

"There's power in stories," Hilda agreed.

Magnus cleared his throat. "Moving on. There's been a troubling influx of subpar mozzarella on the island," Magnus reported in a tone that promised plague and pestilence, not low-quality dairy products. "I spotted the packages in the Apple Cart grocery store. I asked to speak to the manager, but he was unavailable at the time. I'll corner him during the week and come back with a full report at our next meeting."

Brianna had a sneaking suspicion that the manager had encountered Magnus before and had fled the store upon inquiry, but she held her tongue. A glance at Esme's barely concealed smirk confirmed her suspicions.

"Well, I think it's delicious," Hilda said, pulling out a fresh ball of yarn and a pair of oversized shears. "I had some on pizza my daughter cooked up, and it was just lovely. All the guests said so. It melted divinely and stretched for miles. Just a dream. You should try it, Magnus. It's not quite like our local mozzarella, of course, but tasty, nonetheless."

Brianna's heart warmed to tiny Hilda with her bright eyes and chipper voice. In her mind, she'd washed the entire Gourmand Society with a Magnus-style paintbrush, but that wasn't fair or accurate.

Magnus spluttered, but Hilda overrode him without rancor, merely with peppy cheer. "And Brianna, these Danishes are scrumptious. If the rest of your treats are this delightful, the Golden Moon will be the next big thing on Driftwood."

The others nodded and murmured, and Brianna stammered her thanks. That was a much better reception than she'd expected after Magnus's less than warm welcome.

"Moving on," Magnus said loudly. "Susan has a small presentation on the history of mozzarella for us. But before she launches into that, I'd like to discuss the details of our upcoming field trip to see the Montague's water buffalos. We are very fortunate to have a herd on Driftwood Island, allowing cheesemakers to produce *quality* mozzarella for the locals." Magnus threw Hilda a disgruntled look, which was entirely lost on the humming woman flashing her darning needle in and out of a sock.

"Is the field trip still on?" Esme asked. "After the tragedy, and all."

Brianna glanced at Susan to gauge her reaction. She'd clearly heard of the murder, for she looked sorrowful, not shocked. No one at the table showed surprise.

Brianna still wasn't used to the speed of gossip on a small island compared to her old network in the city.

"I contacted Jay as soon as I heard the news," Magnus said.

"With your condolences, I hope." Hilda shot him a stern look, although her fingers never stopped moving.

Magnus shifted in his chair and didn't meet Hilda's eye. "Yes, yes, of course. He said he was still up for the field trip, so we'll meet at Susan's place on Friday at six o'clock, and Jay will join us there to show us the buffalo and give us a milking demonstration."

"Wait." Brianna raised her hand. "So, the Montagues rent land from Susan to house their animals?"

"That's right." Susan raised an eyebrow at Brianna, as if amazed at her presumption at interrupting. Brianna pursed her lips but didn't look away, and Susan continued speaking with clear reluctance. "My land is ideally suited for water buffalo, given the large pond that stays wet even in the driest summer. The Montagues lease the land from me."

Brianna sat back, digesting this information. So, Susan and Owen did have a connection, and a fairly strong one, as landlord and tenant. The two could have been arguing about management of the water buffalo or any number of mundane situations.

However, conflict often followed connection. Brianna glanced at Susan again, who placidly nodded along with Magnus's field trip plans. It would be worth chatting with calm and collected Susan DeVries and seeing what made her tick.

Despite her distraction, Brianna was drawn into the

rest of the meeting. Once Magnus finished pontificating, Susan took over and delivered an engrossing summary of mozzarella history. She spoke of the legends of its origins, when cheese curds accidentally fell into hot water, and the first mention of "mozza" from an Italian monastery in the twelfth century. Brianna hadn't known that water buffalo milk was likely used in the first Italian mozzarella, and she filed it away in the cheese fact drawer in her mind.

At the end of Susan's talk, Esme pulled out a cutting board with a flourish.

"That's a lovely cheese board, Esme," Hilda said.

"It's the work of Sven Janssen, down at the south end." Esme ran her finger along the raw edge of the arbutus board. "A wonderful craftsman. Certainly knows how to handle his wood."

She gave Hilda a knowing look, and the elderly woman tittered. Brianna hid her smile as Quentin looked flustered. Maybe the gossip about Esme from Shaun Bartley had some truth to it, after all. Past the scarves and pungent perfume, Esme had a statuesque figure and striking features, with a personality poised to take advantage of her natural attributes.

Esme pulled out a short cheese knife with a curved wooden handle and a small package. She unwrapped it and sliced off a section for herself before passing it to Quentin.

"Don't worry," she said to Magnus. "It's not the stuff from the Apple Cart that you find so vile. This is local mozzarella made from the Montague's water buffalo milk, the same animals we'll be visiting on Friday."

Magnus harumphed but looked mollified. Brianna accepted the cheese board from Susan and sliced off a piece for herself. The mozzarella was softer than the cow's mozzarella she was used to cooking with and had a lacy look to it. Brianna's slice was delicate on her fingers and creamy on her tongue.

"You can really taste the difference between buffalo and cow mozzarella," Brianna said in the pause while they all chewed. "The buffalo isn't as good to cook with—the water content is higher than cow's—but the flavor is much stronger. Better, in my opinion."

"Quite right," Magnus said in grudging approval. A fleck of forgotten cheese wobbled on his beard. "Glad to hear our newest islander has some ability to discern the finer things in life."

The meeting adjourned soon after the tasting, and Brianna watched Susan's movements carefully while collecting her tin from the table. Susan took a moment to speak to Quentin, then she gathered her purse and sailed out the door like a cruise ship under full steam. Brianna hurried after her.

"Susan," she called to the woman once outside. The sun was low in the sky and cast long shadows from the trees surrounding the community hall. Susan stood in front of her silver sedan, her keys in hand.

Susan turned. Her words were pleasant, but the tone carrying them conveyed surprise that Brianna would dare to hail her. "Brianna, I didn't realize you wanted a word. How can I help you, dear?"

"I wanted to thank you for the mozzarella history lesson," Brianna said truthfully. "It was enlightening. I focus mainly on flavors and how different cheeses hold up under the stress of baking, and I didn't realize how much history has gone into each type."

"I'm glad you enjoyed it," Susan said with a smile, the praise melting her haughtiness. "I'll be honest, I'm no history savant. I spent all yesterday morning from sunrise to coffeetime on the Internet preparing for tonight. That's the sort of procrastination my ex-husband could never abide. Good thing I ousted him." Susan chuckled with a deep, rolling laugh. "My cat was happy enough to lounge on my lap while I searched."

Brianna sucked in her breath. Susan's alibi for yesterday morning wasn't strong, if only her cat could corroborate it. Could this woman have killed Owen? A glance at her sturdy arms and competent face told Brianna that it was a possibility, but did Susan have a motive?

"Furry blankets are great company," Brianna agreed. Her mind wandered to the idea of a companion for herself since the float home felt a little empty. Zola crossed her mind, but a float home was no place for a grazing animal. Would a cat like living on the docks? She forced herself to pay attention to the conversation. "Terrible news about the murder of Owen yesterday morning, isn't it? I'd never met him, but it must be a shock to a tight-knit community like Driftwood Island. You must have known him since his water buffalo are on your land."

"Oh, yes," Susan agreed without emotion behind her words. "A tragedy, indeed, especially for Tansy and young Jay."

"I don't have a good sense of the man," Brianna said. "I get conflicting reports from everyone. What was your opinion of Owen?"

Susan stared at her for a moment, and Brianna wondered if she had pushed the snooty woman too far. Then Susan glanced around to make sure no one was exiting the hall within earshot.

"Between you and me," she said quietly, "he wasn't the easiest man to get along with. I had to deal with him, since the Montagues lease my pond, but I didn't enjoy it. He could be very confrontational, unless you were a beautiful woman, of course."

She threw Brianna a knowing look. Brianna tensed her muscles. How could she probe further now that Susan was willingly confiding in her?

"Yes, Esme mentioned that he was yelling at you in the parking lot of the Apple Cart," Brianna said in a sympathetic voice. She deliberately phrased her words to take any censure off Susan in the former confrontation. "That must have been upsetting. Was he overreacting? Men like that often get angry over the smallest things."

Susan nodded vigorously. "That was Owen to a T." She paused, searching for words. "I politely asked him to not park on my lawn when he came to check the buffalo—there's plenty of parking on the driveway, but still he always dug his front tires into my grass—and he didn't take it well."

Brianna sighed inwardly. Susan seemed too calm to engage in a fit of passion, but she could plan a calculated assault. Brianna still didn't see a motive for Susan killing Owen, but the confrontation smelled of deceit. If they had truly fought over Owen's parking mishap, Brianna would eat Esme's cheese board.

Susan lowered her voice, and Brianna leaned forward to catch her words. "Can I tell you something?" the older woman whispered. "I don't believe Dot Dubois killed Owen."

Chapter 13

Brianna's breath hitched. She stared at Susan, half of whose face was lit with the orangey glow of the setting sun, half in deep shadows. It was vindicating to hear her own opinion coming from someone else's mouth. But if Susan were the killer, why wouldn't she latch onto the easiest solution? Dot was already in custody. Unless she had another, stronger suspect in mind.

"Why do you think that?" Brianna whispered back. "I'd love to see Dot Dubois's name cleared, if she really didn't kill Owen." Brianna hadn't mentioned that Dot was her aunt, and despite the gossip that freely flew between islanders, Susan hadn't seemed to realize their connection.

"Owen wasn't without his demons." Susan waved her hand in a dismissive gesture. "He was wrapped up in something shady. I won't bore you with the details, but his past was bound to come back to haunt him."

Susan waited a moment while Magnus stumped down the porch steps and toward an ancient pickup truck in the parking lot. Brianna fidgeted, waiting for the older man to get in his vehicle. Once the door slammed shut, Susan continued to speak.

"There's a new man in town," she said. "Hilda told me. He's staying at her bed and breakfast, the Bumblebee B&B." Susan shook her head with a slow, knowing expression. "Hilda's establishment often attracts the wrong sort. It's likely the substandard food they pump out. I wouldn't eat there if my life depended on it. Anyway, Hilda said the new man is shady as all get-out. Gave her the creeps, she said, and she's tolerant of everyone. Hilda said he and Owen were talking in her back lane, and it got heated." Susan tapped her nose. "If you ask me, Owen's past caught up with him. It was only a matter of time. You can't outrun what you are."

Well, there's a depressing notion, Brianna thought. What was the point of trying to reinvent herself on Driftwood Island if she couldn't let go of her past? She hoped Susan wasn't correct, although her tale of the mystery man at the B&B was intriguing.

However, it also stank of misdirection. Susan was hiding plenty, and her alibi wasn't nearly strong enough to dissuade Brianna of her suspect status. In fact, depending on what she was hiding, Susan might be her prime suspect.

Hilda Button had witnessed the altercations between the new man and Owen as well as Owen and Susan. While Brianna wanted to look suspiciously at Hilda, she couldn't do so with a straight face. The elderly woman was fit enough to darn her socks, but if she had the strength to shove a pitchfork in someone's back, Brianna would be heartily surprised. Besides, Hilda would have been at Happy Hearts preschool at the time of the murder, dropping her granddaughter off. Brianna could check with Macy easily enough.

Unfortunately, she still didn't have any evidence pointing directly to Susan, and she didn't want to go to Devon Moore and the Mounties again without any.

She'd had enough of Devon putting her in her place, and she didn't hold high hopes for unknown detectives from the Major Crime Unit listening to her theories. Being put in her place wasn't a comfortable feeling, since that was the exact bit of her past with Greg that she was trying to forget. No, she wouldn't bother the Mounties until she had something tangible.

"Intriguing," she said aloud. "The deeper one digs, the more secrets pop out of the closet."

Susan burst out with her belly laugh again. "Quite right. Be careful where you dig." She nodded to Brianna. "Good luck with your café preparations, and keep your shovel in the toolshed where it belongs."

Still chuckling, Susan strode purposefully to her car and left the parking lot with a wave. Brianna stared after the vehicle, her mind whirling. Was the comment about the shovel meant as a warning? Brianna shivered and walked toward the road and her float home. She'd had enough of all this intrigue. Investigations would have to wait until tomorrow to resume.

Brianna pulled up to the police station at exactly nine o'clock the next morning. She rested her bicycle against the wall and presented herself at the front desk.

"I would like to visit Dorothy Dubois," she said clearly to the officer behind the counter, who looked up at Brianna over her glasses with a waiting expression. "I was told she could have visitors this morning."

The woman nodded and handed her a clipboard. "Good thing you came now. She's going to be transferred this afternoon. Sign the visitor's log here. And I'll need to see some ID."

Brianna filled in the form and passed her driver's license to the officer. When she was satisfied, the woman rose from her chair and directed her to a side door. It led to a short hallway. Through a half-open door, she caught a glimpse of Devon Moore and a paunchy man with baggy eyes and a shrewd expression talking intently. Was that one of the detectives from the Major Crime Unit? Brianna swallowed and brought her eyes forward. Halfway down the hallway, the woman opened a door to a small interrogation room.

"Wait here," the officer said.

Brianna entered the room, furnished only by a table bolted to the floor and two chairs. The woman closed the door behind her, and Brianna perched gingerly on the chair that wasn't in front of a metal loop in the tabletop.

She waited with growing impatience, but it was a full ten minutes before the door opened again and Dot shuffled in. Brianna scraped back her chair and stood to greet her aunt. Dot was dressed in the same clothes she'd been wearing when arrested, although their wrinkles were now pronounced after two nights of sleeping in them. Her graying hair was lank and flat, and her face was free of makeup. She looked tired and drawn with prominent black circles under her eyes, and Brianna hardly recognized the vibrant aunt she knew.

"Stay seated, please," the Mountie ordered Brianna. She locked Dot's handcuffed hands to the table. "No touching. Your meeting will be monitored. Knock on the door when you're ready to leave."

She left, and Brianna sank into her seat again, staring at her aunt. Dot tried to smile, but it was a shadow of her usual joie de vivre.

"How are you?" Brianna whispered. The words sounded inane to her ears, but she needed to know that Dot was okay.

"I'm fine, child," Dot said. "They're treating me just fine. They'll be transferring me to a corrections facility on the mainland soon, until my trial. I should get a snazzy new outfit there."

Brianna bit her lip, frustrated at the whole situation. Why was Dot even here?

"What really happened?" she hissed. "Why did you confess to Owen's murder? I know you didn't do it."

Something flashed in Dot's eyes, some hint of her former fire, then it faded, and Dot smiled wistfully.

"I wish I hadn't," she said. "It was stupid, impetuous. Of course, I regret it terribly. I just got so angry at Owen's threat to move the stream that feeds my pond. What would Zola and I do without it? And he and I have had a rocky relationship for years. This was the straw that broke the camel's back, that's all."

A scowl of true emotion crossed Dot's face, and Brianna wondered for a second whether her trust in her aunt was misplaced. Then she shook herself. The two might have been at odds, but Dot would never have killed Owen Montague. It just wasn't in her to take a life, no matter how impulsive she was.

"I don't believe you," Brianna said with a scowl to match her aunt's. "And I'm going to prove you didn't kill Owen. Even if you're willing to take the fall for something you didn't do, I'm not willing to let you."

"Drop it, Brianna." Dot's eyes flashed with anger and fear. "Please, let it go. I'm old enough to make my own bed and lie in it. Go, live your life, set up your café, and let me face the consequences of my actions."

Brianna stared at her aunt for a long moment. Why was Dot doing this? Was she covering up for someone else? But who was important enough to Dot—more important than being present for her own niece—that she would take the fall for murder? What—or who—was Dot hiding?

"I moved here on your advice," Brianna said, her voice wavering. She took a deep breath to calm herself. "Remember that night after Greg died, when we drank too much wine and you brought out flyers from the realtor's office? You sold me on a dream, one where I could start a new life in Snuggler's Cove. One where I could stop by for tea with my favorite aunt." Brianna waved around the interrogation room. "I really thought I'd be sailing on Guster with you this summer, not visiting you at the Mountie station."

Dot's eyes were filled with tears. "I'm sorry, child," she said quietly. "I wanted that too."

Dot still wouldn't tell her the secret she was hiding, even after Brianna had poured out her heart. What else could she do?

"Make sure your lawyer knows to call on me as a

witness. Character reference? I don't know, however I can help."

"I don't have a lawyer," Dot said. "I'll just use the crown-appointed one. I'm guilty, after all."

"Are you kidding?" Brianna stared at her aunt. "I have some savings. If it's cash flow you're worried about, we can figure it out."

"Leave it, child." Dot heaved a massive sigh. "Please, just let me be."

"I'm going to figure out what's really going on." Brianna stood, her stomach churning with frustration. "You might not care about yourself, but I do."

Brianna and Macy clinked glasses at the Stumbling Goose pub that evening after Brianna's long day of baking and creating promotional materials for the café. Staff were setting up a microphone in the corner for an open mic night, but no one had yet taken the stage. Macy sipped her rosé wine and sighed happily.

"Thanks for getting me out," she said. "It doesn't happen often enough. I missed out on a lot of this sort of thing when Oaklyn was young. Then when she was old enough to leave alone, everyone else my age was busy."

"I'm happy you agreed to come. I'm not exactly rolling in social engagements here, as the newcomer, and I'm counting on you to fill up my severely lacking social calendar."

Macy laughed and popped a fry between her lips. Brianna eyed her burger and wondered how she would fit the towering monster into her mouth. Fresh tomatoes and crispy lettuce hung out above a thick, juicy patty, and sauce dripped onto Brianna's plate when she held the burger up. Her mouth watered, and she took a bite of the edge as best as she could. Savory flavors burst in her mouth, and she chewed slowly to extract every morsel of tastiness.

"How are you doing, anyway?" Macy said, an uncharacteristically serious expression on her face. She marred it slightly by shoving another fry in her mouth. "Ugh, the fries are so good here. But seriously, it hasn't been very long since Greg passed away. You seem fine on the surface, but what's going on in here?" She tapped her own chest for emphasis.

Brianna put down her burger. Its sheer size needed her full concentration which she couldn't give it if Macy were going to delve into deep topics.

"Surprisingly okay," she said. When Macy shot her a disbelieving look, she elaborated. "Don't get me wrong, I miss him dreadfully. But honestly, I miss the idea of him more than the reality. We were pretty rocky near the end. I miss early-years Greg, when he would surprise me with sneaky hugs in the kitchen when my back was turned. I miss having another presence in the house. I miss having someone to talk to at the end of the day." Brianna swirled a fry in her ketchup. "But I don't miss the needling, the disparaging comments, the putdowns that were growing more and more frequent until I felt small and stupid almost all the time."

Brianna lifted her eyes to meet Macy's sympathetic ones. Macy reached out and clasped Brianna's hand in her own. Brianna huffed a little laugh.

"It sounds terrible to say these things about a dead man," she said. "I wouldn't tell them to anyone but you."

Macy made a sign of zipping her lips shut. "Your secrets are always safe with me. Besides, who would I tell? It's not like my boyfriend situation is rosy." Macy squeezed Brianna's hand and released it to take a drink. "The perils of living on a small island, I'm afraid. But I'm stuck here now, at least until Oaklyn is out of the house. She's settled here, and I have my job—which I love—so we're not going anywhere." She sighed dramatically. "I'll have to settle for book boyfriends instead."

"Those never let you down," Brianna said, and they clinked their glasses together.

"Brianna?" a familiar voice said.

Chapter 14

Brianna twisted her head toward the familiar voice speaking her name. Devon Moore stood near their table, a look of surprise on his face. He was dressed in jeans and a slim-fitting black tee shirt that set off his dark hair. His shirt held droplets of water from the late-spring rain that was tapering off outside. This was the first time Brianna had seen the Mountie in anything other than a uniform, and he wore his casual clothes very well indeed.

His eyes drifted over Brianna, then they snapped back to her face. Brianna nodded at him, surprised he'd called her out. He must have shocked himself, because his expression told her he hadn't thought out his next words.

"I'm glad to see you're not dwelling," he said, shifting the handle of an instrument case from one hand to the other. He stared at Brianna, and she glanced at the case to avoid his intense gaze. Was he planning to play tonight? "On the investigation, I mean. We have it under control, I promise you that."

Devon's words might have been meant kindly, but Brianna bristled. After speaking with Macy about Greg's foibles, her healing wounds were too raw to listen to Devon's words without reacting.

"I'm looking forward to hearing when you've tracked down another suspect," she said pointedly. "Let me know when Dot Dubois can come home."

Devon's mouth set in a thin line, but he was spared

from answering by the arrival of the hostess. He followed the woman with one last glance at Brianna and a nod in their direction. Brianna didn't speak until he had disappeared around a corner of the pub.

"Wow," Macy said, fanning her face. "The words were harsh, but the chemistry was hot. How do you manage to attract the most eligible bachelor on the island after a month, when I can barely scrape together a handful of dates in as many years?"

"Chemistry?" Brianna wrinkled her nose at Macy. "Don't even get me started. What a tool. He wants me to stop investigating the murder like a good little woman. Know your place. Well, forget that. I've uncovered more in the past few days than the entire detachment is willing to entertain."

Macy leaned forward, her eyes gleaming. "Tell me more. What have you found out?"

"Where do I begin? Shaun is still a suspect, of course. Owen being his romantic rival is strong motive, and he doesn't have an alibi yet. Shaun mentioned Esmerelda Alonso, and I spoke to her at the Gourmand Society meeting. Again, her alibi is weak, and there's something she's hiding about her relationship with Owen. She said Owen pursued her and she turned him down, but I smelled a lie in there somewhere."

"I wouldn't put it past her." Macy bit into her burger and chewed thoughtfully. A guitarist tapped the microphone in the corner and mumbled a few words before launching into an old folk song. "She's impulsive and emotional. And I'd bet that there's more to that rejection story than she told you."

"I wanted to check with you. Was Hilda Button at your preschool the morning of the murder?"

"Hilda? For sure. She talked my ear off for a solid half hour while I was wrangling the children." Macy snorted. "Why? Were you seriously suspecting her?"

Brianna sighed with a rueful smile. "Just covering my bases. As for a suspect, it could still be Tansy or Jay Montague, but I don't have any evidence of a motive for either of them. My current working theory is Susan DeVries." Brianna kept her voice low, thankful for the privacy their booth afforded them. "There was bad blood between her and Owen, I'm sure of it. Hilda saw them arguing in the grocery store parking lot. And Susan was quick enough to point fingers in another direction, something that felt like grasping at straws."

"She's composed enough to plan out a murder," Macy said. "I've never seen her raise her voice, which makes me wonder exactly what she and Owen were arguing about. If they had fought, she wouldn't get mad afterward, she'd get even. I heard once that someone on the west side wanted to subdivide their property. Susan lives nearby, and the other homeowner crashed his car into her fence a year before, so the story goes, and didn't offer to pay for damages. Although Susan didn't leave traces of her involvement, the subdivision plans fell through from pressure from the neighborhood." Macy leaned forward. "Then, to make matters worse, every offer that the homeowner got after they put their place on sale was rescinded until they had to accept a sale price well below asking. If Susan's hand wasn't in that, I'll eat my napkin."

Brianna shivered. That was the sort of woman who could stab someone in the back, literally and figuratively.

"I think we need to find out more about Susan," she said.

Macy slapped the table. "Yes. I can do that. Leave it to me. I'll have her secrets wormed out in no time." In her sweet, talking-to-kids voice, Macy said, "No one can resist the charms of the innocent preschool teacher."

Brianna raised her glass again, and they toasted.

"To revealing secrets," Brianna said.

"And Dot's safe return," Macy agreed.

The guitarist finished his song, and the boisterous pubgoers clapped and whistled. Grinning with shy joy, the guitarist stumbled away from the microphone and slumped in a nearby chair with his laughing friends who pushed a beer toward him. The next performer strode with purposeful steps toward the microphone.

"I didn't know Devon played the violin," Macy said in a hushed voice. She kicked Brianna under the table. "Did you?"

"How on earth would I know that?" Brianna stared at Devon, who loosely held his violin in one hand with the ease of someone either well-versed in the instrument or with no clue of its value. He leaned into the microphone to speak.

"Evening, everyone. I have a traditional pub tune for you tonight. I hope you've drunk enough to excuse any squeaks my fiddle makes."

The crowd laughed and clapped their encouragement. Brianna waited with all-consuming interest. Devon pushed the microphone aside and held his instrument under his chin. With a practiced motion, he brought the bow to the strings.

His arm launched into a frenzy of motion, drawing forth a riotous explosion of sound. Brianna's jaw dropped. Did all those notes come from one single instrument? If she'd heard this on the radio, she would have assumed two fiddles were playing, at least.

"Wow, he's good," Macy said with awe. "Who knew what our officious officer was capable of?"

Devon's face was intense in its concentration, but he occasionally glanced around while he played, and his eyes crinkled with the hint of a smile. The tune was infectious, and Brianna's toe tapped along with the clapping rhythm of the patrons around her.

When he finished the tune, he flung his bow down and gave a short, sharp bow. The pub patrons cheered wildly, and Brianna brought her hands together in true appreciation. Devon might be too keen on putting her in her place, but she appreciated his talent.

"He could play my fiddle anytime," Macy said with a giggle and clinked her wine glass against Brianna's. She coughed. "Ugh, Cecilia's moving in for the kill, look."

A woman with sleek black hair, a finely sculpted face, and a tight skirt sashayed toward Devon, who was placing his fiddle back in its case. She pushed her petite frame close to him and leaned toward his ear to speak over the noise of the pub.

"That's Cecelia, the one you told me was chatting Devon up before?" Brianna took a sip of her drink and watched the drama unfolding. Her mind wanted to enjoy the gossip blossoming before her eyes—Hilda Button would be agog to hear, she was sure—but her stomach twisted oddly. She ignored the frustration that heated her chest and attributed it to her general annoyance with Devon.

"That's her. Oh, isn't she a friendly one?" Macy scoffed and shook her head. Cecilia had put her hand on Devon's arm and was now pulling him gently to follow her. Devon, for his part, looked bewildered but interested. Macy sighed. "So much for your chemistry. You'll have to get your claws sharpened if you want to fight Cecilia for her prey."

"What makes you think I want to fight for Devon Moore?" Brianna said. Macy rolled her eyes, and Brianna gritted her teeth. "He sounds as bad as Greg. I don't need that in my life right now. I want to be me for a while, unencumbered by men telling me what to do. Cecilia can have the pompous pig."

"That was harsh but very empowered." Macy raised her glass, and Brianna clinked it with a firm gesture. "To solitary solidarity."

The next day, Brianna held a paintbrush in her hand. Yellow dripped off the end while she admired her handiwork. The Golden Moon was shaping up to be as pleasing in real life as it was in her imagination. The yellow interior walls now drew the eye of any passerby. A green and white striped awning provided shade from the warming late-spring sun after the rains of yesterday, and large black lettering clearly proclaimed the café's name in the window. Sunlight warmed Brianna's back as she basked in the view.

Her smile slipped off her face. She wished Dot were here to see the café. Even after giving her clues to Devon—who hopefully had passed on the message to the detectives—Dot had been transferred to the corrections facility on the mainland. Granted, the police had no other suspects, and Dot insisted on the truth of her confession. Still, Brianna chafed at her aunt's incarceration.

It was mid-morning, but she was working at the café because Shaun had called, saying he wouldn't make it in today. She had carefully avoided staying in the café alone with him, so she welcomed a chance to get some painting done without his looming presence.

Hilda Button approached with the shuffling gait of the elderly. A sock dangled out of the large purse that hung off her shoulder, ready to be darned at the slightest opportunity. Brianna raised her hand to wave but faltered at the look on Hilda's face. The older woman hurried closer.

"Oh, Brianna, have you heard the news?" Hilda put a hand on her panting chest. "It's terrible."

"What happened?" Brianna took Hilda's arm and propelled her through the café's open door. A wooden chair held a pencil and a tape measure, but Brianna swept them away and lowered Hilda onto it. "Tell me what's wrong."

"It's Susan," Hilda said. "Susan DeVries. She's dead."

Brianna stepped back in shock. She'd spoken to Susan only two days ago at the meeting of the Gourmand Society. How could she be dead?

"How did she die?"

"Oh, it's simply tragic. Such a meaningless accident." Hilda's hand fluttered near her face with her emotion. "The newspaper delivery girl found her trampled to death in the water buffalo field. What she was doing there, I have no idea. She couldn't stand the creatures and always gave their field a wide berth. And rightly so, given how she died. Death by buffalo stampede, can you imagine? What a terrible way to go."

"Trampled by water buffalo," Brianna repeated. "And you say she never usually entered their field?"

"No, never. That's why it was so odd." Hilda took a handkerchief out of her sleeve and blew her nose loudly. "Such a loss."

Brianna couldn't help noticing the lack of moist eyes that accompanied Hilda's nose-blowing antics. The woman struck her as an incurable gossip, maybe more interested in telling her the news than mourning Susan's death. From what Brianna had heard and seen of Susan, she didn't blame Hilda's lack of sincerity.

"I'm sorry to hear that," Brianna said. "Can I offer you some tea?"

"No, no, thank you, dear." Hilda stood with effort. "Places to go, people to see. Oh my, I suppose Beatrice at the clothing boutique won't have heard the news yet. I'd better break it to her gently." Her eyes gleamed in anticipation over spreading the news further. "I wonder if our field trip to see the water buffalo will be canceled.

I should speak to Magnus."

She tottered out of the café, and Brianna leaned against the doorway to digest the news of Susan's passing. Her death, so soon after Owen's, felt too connected to be a coincidence. That, paired with Susan's dislike of the buffalo roaming her property, and Brianna's suspicions were aroused. What if Susan's death wasn't a tragic accident, and instead was another murder by the same killer who had stabbed Owen?

It was too likely to ignore. Brianna stood straight and dipped her paintbrush in a can of water. She would clean up later. For now, she had a crime scene to examine.

If Susan wasn't the killer, that meant someone else was, and that person was desperate enough to strike twice.

Chapter 15

Brianna washed her hands, stuffed a few plastic baggies in her pocket, then hopped on her bike, too curious to bother changing her clothes into something less paint-smeared. With any luck, she wouldn't see anyone on her clandestine mission to examine the scene of Susan's death.

It took her multiple checks of her phone's map and Magnus's emailed directions to find Susan's property on the western side of the island. The Gourmand Society was supposed to meet there tonight for their field trip, otherwise Brianna wouldn't have had a clue where Susan lived.

She pedaled along a twisty road that skirted Mt. Dashton, the largest peak on the island covered in patches of bald rock jutting out of a thick blanket of conifers. Fanciful mailboxes dotted the roadway made of welded chains and carved logs in the shape of pirate heads, and dirt driveways wended through trees on either side. It was a pleasant ride in the dappled sunlight filtering through tree branches above, but Brianna wouldn't have wanted to ride through here in the dark.

The trees thinned and gave way to farmland on the west side of Mt. Dashton, with sloping fields that drifted into the ocean beyond. Brianna took a deep breath of sea air and coasted down the road toward a good-sized pond glittering in the afternoon sun. Large black animals with horns waded in the water, and Brianna smiled. Here were the fabled water buffalos, at last.

A plain, serviceable mailbox with a sign of metal letters affixed on a painted board announced the DeVries property. Brianna glanced down the dirt track, but no cars or signs of company presented themselves, so she cautiously wheeled down the driveway. The track split early on, with one way leading to a modest yet well-kept modern house topped by a new roof equipped with solar panels, and expensive-looking landscaping. The other wandered to a fenced field enclosing a pond where the water buffalos lived. A large barn stood adjacent to the fencing, and Brianna swung off her bike and pushed it into the shadows of a tractor on the far side.

Brianna had no idea what she was looking for, but she wouldn't find anything by not searching. She scouted around the dirt driveway first, after glancing warily at the road for oncoming visitors. The soft dirt, which must have been damp that morning from dew and yesterday afternoon's rain, had hardened with the early summer's sun.

Brianna narrowed her eyes. Multiple vehicles had parked here in recent days. Two tracks were the same and were likely police cruisers. Another larger vehicle might be an ambulance, and Brianna pulled out her phone to snap pictures of the tire tracks impressed in the dried mud. She could match them up to the vehicles later if she had a reason to. It was better to record evidence before it disappeared with a spring squall.

She glanced over the tracks in front of the barn one more time after taking pictures, and her sharp eyes zeroed in on a single, different track. The police cruiser tires had almost obliterated signs of it, but one short stretch showed the new track clearly. Brianna snapped a photo then peered at the track with interest. It was odd, with each side of the tread appearing different. She recalled Greg mentioning that asymmetrical tires were great for high-performance automobiles—his hobby had been drooling over expensive sports cars—and Brianna wondered who was driving around this vehicle on Driftwood Island. From what she remembered of Susan's car after seeing it drive away after the Gourmand Society meeting, it was the typical midrange sedan parked in front of Susan's house.

Brianna didn't know where this information might lead, but all evidence was worthy of documenting. Someone other than the police and Susan had been here after the rains of Thursday afternoon. It might mean nothing, but it might mean foul play.

Brianna pushed open the sturdy wooden gate and entered the water buffalo enclosure. She glanced nervously at the water buffalos near their pond, but they continued to munch grass without paying her much attention. She breathed a relieved sigh and scanned the soft ground for more signs.

Multiple boot prints led from the gate to the middle of the field, closer to the pond. Brianna followed them slowly with one eye on the water buffalos. The footprints stopped at a churned-up patch of bare dirt in the grass field. Hoofprints were so numerous as to be scarcely indistinguishable from each other, but the boots walked on top of them and around a flattened area of mud the size of a body lying down. Brianna swallowed hard. That must have been where they'd found Susan's body.

To distract herself from the morbid reality of what she was doing here, Brianna glanced away from the smooth, drying mud and looked around the scene. Clearly, water buffalos had trampled this area, so death by stampede was not a bad assumption. But could Brianna deduce anything else from the dirt? She paced around the trampled patch, scanning clumps of grass for anything out of place.

She'd almost given up when a flash of white caught her eye. She grabbed a baggie out of her pocket and pushed it inside out. With her fingers in the bag, she plucked the piece of paper out of the mud. She carefully held it aloft to read.

It was a receipt, and Brianna's heart pattered in her chest. A receipt in the middle of the field? The only people who could have dropped it were the emergency workers, Owen or Jay Montague, Susan DeVries, or the erstwhile murderer. Since Owen and Susan were both dead and Brianna could firmly rule them out as suspects, that left Jay or an unknown.

She peered at the text, searching for clues. Someone had bought a smoothie and a muffin at the Bumblebee Sunday morning and paid in cash. Brianna's fingers tightened on the receipt. Hilda Button owned the B&B. Would she remember who had bought something that morning? It was worthwhile asking her. It hadn't been Susan, Brianna was certain of that. Susan had made her disdain for the B&B's food clear.

Brianna straightened with resolve. If this wasn't a

strong piece of evidence that Susan's death wasn't an accident, she didn't know what was. If the deaths of Susan and Owen were connected, and they could prove it, then Dot would be exonerated.

After tucking the bag-covered receipt in her pocket, Brianna jogged to her bicycle and threw herself onto it. Was this enough evidence to get the detectives thinking harder about these cases? She needed to find out. Her legs pumped the pedals along the dirt driveway and back up the winding road around Mt. Dashton.

She was winded by the time her bike jolted over a speedbump in the town hall's parking lot where all the island's official services resided. Brianna examined the tires of police cruisers as she cycled past, and each one had symmetrical treads. The mystery tracks she'd seen at Susan's weren't from the police. The glass door to the Mounties' office stood open to encourage fresh air to enter, and Brianna stepped in.

Brianna recognized Constable Lenox from her aunt's arrest. He looked up from the front desk with a bored expression.

"Is Corporal Devon Moore around?" Brianna asked Lenox. She didn't want to divulge her tenuous evidence and theories to anyone else. For all of Devon's insistence on her leaving the case alone, she felt he would listen to her without immediately brushing her off. He would warn her away, she expected, but he wouldn't laugh.

"Moore," Lenox called over his shoulder. "Someone here for you."

Devon ducked out of a back room, clutching a cup of coffee in one hand and a file folder in the other. His warm brown eyes glanced at Brianna and widened in surprise.

"Ms. West," he said. "How can I help you?"

"I'd like to speak to you," Brianna said. Her fingers clenched the baggie, and Devon's eyes fell on it then flicked up to her face again. She made a half-glance at Lenox. "In private."

"Come on in," he said, waving her forward without hesitation.

Brianna followed Devon, happy to escape the curious eyes of Lenox. Devon touched her elbow to guide her into a small room with tables and chairs lined against one side. The Mounties must have used it as an all-purpose room. He released Brianna's arm quickly as if he hadn't meant to touch her, and turned to her once the door closed.

"I found evidence," she blurted out before he could speak. "About Susan DeVries's death. I don't think it was an accident, and I think it's connected to the murder of Owen Montague."

Devon's eyebrows rose until they almost brushed a dark lock that had escaped the stiff waves of the rest of his hair. He glanced again at the baggie.

"What did you find?"

Brianna held out her evidence, and Devon took the baggie, his eyes scanning the receipt through the plastic with a frown.

"It's for the Bumblebee, Sunday morning," she said in a rush. "You know, the morning of Owen Montague's murder. I found it at the site of Susan's death, in her water buffalo field. It was trampled into the dirt, so it's not just a piece of trash that blew in. It could have been from an emergency worker's pocket, I suppose, but someone else had visited the barn between the rains on Thursday afternoon and the arrival of ambulances and police cruisers, because I found tire tracks that didn't match either of those. I'm pretty sure they don't match Jay Montague's truck, either, but you could check that. Someone was there, in that field, someone other than Susan or the Montagues taking care of their water buffalos. Given that Susan had an altercation with Owen on Saturday, she was the person he leased land from, and she accused him of having a shady past, there are too many connections to ignore. I'm not sure how the pieces fit together yet, but there is too much coincidence to pretend that Susan's death was an accident. She hated the water buffalos. What was she doing in their field?"

Brianna paused after her unburdening of clues. It felt good to get them off her chest. Devon stared at her with a faint frown creasing his smooth brow.

"Thank you for coming forward with this," he said finally, his fingers gripping the receipt firmly. "In fact, we have an anonymous tip with an eyewitness account of another suspect leaving the area at the time of Owen Montague's death, so the detectives will cross-check our information. I promise, they will practice due diligence in their investigation. But please, allow the detectives to do their jobs. You shouldn't be poking around other people's properties without permission, hunting for clues. I understand you want to exonerate your aunt, but you need to let the Major Crime Unit handle this without interference."

Brianna's lips tightened as heat rose in her chest. Again, Devon was shutting her down. Every time he did it, she hated it more and more. She didn't want to be the person who replied with a meek "yes, dear" anymore. She was a new person on this island, or at least was trying to be, and falling into the ruts of her old life was beyond aggravating.

"As soon as you start taking things seriously, I will back off," she said with crisp annunciation, biting back the harsher words she longed to throw at him. "Please let me know when Dot Dubois has been released so I can pick her up. Now that another murder has occurred—likely connected—you know it couldn't possibly have been her."

Brianna left without a backward glance. Devon didn't try to stop her, and Lenox merely stared as she passed. Brianna marched to her bike and yanked the front tire toward the road. She didn't need Corporal Devon Moore. She had eyes to see and a mouth to speak with. She could gather more evidence—irrefutable evidence—that proved beyond a shadow of a doubt that Dot was innocent, confession or not. With that in mind, Brianna pushed off the curb toward the Bumblebee. She needed answers, and Hilda Button was the font of islander knowledge.

Chapter 16

The parking lot of the Bumblebee was almost full when Brianna leaned her bike against a fence separating cars from the neighboring field of sheep. The picket fence didn't obstruct the gorgeous view of a tiny bay that cupped the ocean between forested arms of land. The Bumblebee was a grand house, three levels high, that featured brick siding, multiple peaked roofs with a round turret, and a semi-circular porch with white railings that oozed with homey invitation. A long one-level addition jutted out from the main building and housed the B&B's restaurant.

Inside the restaurant's door, an entryway with a potted plant opened into a bright and cheery dining room filled with round tables covered in pastel pink and green tablecloths and vases with a single pink rose in each. Hilda was sitting in one of two comfortable armchairs beside a floor-to-ceiling window with the light streaming in. A patron left her as Brianna approached, looking dazed, and Hilda greeted Brianna with a bright smile.

"Brianna, my dear, how good to see you. Sit, sit. Would you like a cup of tea? No? Well, put your feet up, anyway."

Brianna sank into the squashy armchair across from Hilda with a sigh. The day had been an active one, to say the least. Now that she had stopped, her leg muscles ached from her bike riding, and her shoulders were tight from the stress of investigation. She must have looked tired because Hilda clucked her tongue.

"You look tuckered out, my dear. What's wrong?"

Was there any point in dancing around the issue? Brianna couldn't muster up the energy to find a reason.

"Do you know who might have bought a smoothie and muffin on Sunday morning? I found a receipt from the B&B restaurant, and I need to know whose it is."

Hilda looked thoughtful. "We have plenty of visitors at that time, and smoothies are the reason people come, mainly. I can have a think."

"Would Susan have bought it, do you think?"

Hilda laughed loudly then covered her mouth with a look of horror.

"I'm sorry," she said. "That was rude, laughing about a dead woman. Poor Susan. But she always made it perfectly clear what she thought of our smoothies. She wasn't shy with her words, she wasn't." Hilda's lips pursed. Clearly, Susan's blatant dismissal of the Bumblebee's offerings had never sat well with the elderly woman. "No, Susan never darkened the restaurant's doors, and certainly not for a smoothie."

Brianna tucked that information away. The receipt wasn't Susan's, that was almost certain.

"What about Jay Montague?" she said. What other suspects did she have? "Tansy Montague? Esmerelda Alonso? Shaun Bartley?"

"Oh, my," Hilda said with a comfortable sigh. Her fingers worked tirelessly on the sock she was darning. This one had a jazzy pattern of yellow stars on a purple background. "Let me see. Young Jay doesn't come in much, and I didn't see Tansy or Esme, but they could have come in while I was upstairs, it's entirely possible. Shaun was in, I do remember that. He's a regular, for sure. I have a solid set of regulars. The islanders are creatures of habit. Not that I blame them! If I don't pop into the post office every day, they phone and check to make sure I'm still kicking."

Brianna tried not to react to Hilda's comment about Shaun, but all her muscles tensed. She mentally moved Shaun to the top of her suspect list again.

"And that new fellow was here," Hilda rabbited on, unaware of Brianna's distraction. "He's been here for a few days, now. The other guests tend to try out new restaurants, but he's eaten here or bought food to go for every meal since he arrived last week." She gave Brianna a knowing glance. "He's an odd duck, that one. Keeps himself to himself, he does." She tilted her head while she thought. "Pearce, I think his last name was. Yes, Connor Pearce. I remember because he signed the guestbook. I insist that every guest signs—my daughter rolls her eyes at that, but I ran this place for years, and I still know a thing or two. The guestbook lets us see where everyone is from, and it makes the guests think about the best aspects of their visit, which helps them remember it in a better light." She chuckled then looked thoughtful. "That's why I remembered Connor Pearce. He wrote down his hometown as Sechelt, which isn't a place that many guests record."

Brianna focused on the older woman with interest. She'd heard of Sechelt before, mainly because her aunt

Dot had lived in the small town for a time during her teen years before Brianna was born. Family lore had it as a work experience gig, working for a few months at a fishing lodge that a family friend owned.

"Is this Connor guy around today?" Brianna asked. "I've never been to Sechelt and wouldn't mind chatting to him about it."

"Oh, he was here a moment ago." Hilda put her hands on her armrests and leaned around her chair to search the dining room. "Yes, there he is, at the counter. See? With the ballcap?"

Brianna bit her lip. Connor Pearce fit the description of "scruffy" better than anyone she'd ever met. Three-day-old stubble covered his chin and cheeks, and his tee shirt's collar was frayed above a washed-out logo. His crow's feet and leathery skin spoke of a life lived hard, even though his sandy blond hair hadn't yet been touched by white. He scowled at his wallet like it owed him.

Connor had arrived last week, the same time as the newcomer Susan DeVries had mentioned, and he would certainly classify as a shady character in Susan's estimation. Was this the man that Owen had argued with?

"I'm sorry to hear about your aunt," Hilda said, pulling Brianna's attention back to the other woman. Her fingers continued their incessant darning. "Such a shock. I can't believe that she'd do such a thing. I'm sure there's been some misunderstanding, and we'll all be laughing about it in a month." Her face clouded over. "Well, everyone except Owen and his family. But if it is true, I wouldn't blame her, not entirely. Of course, murder is a step too far, but Dot had cause to be angry at the development coming her way."

"What development?" Brianna had seen the excavator, but all Dot had told her was that Owen had planned to redirect the stream into the storm drain at the front of his property, bypassing Dot's pond altogether.

"I heard it from Alicia Marley. She's the realtor in town, I assume you met her when you bought your place. She said that Owen Montague was planning to sell his property to a company who was going to develop the land into a golf course, of all things. They needed to redirect the stream, and Dot wouldn't see a lick of water, nor any of the money that the Montagues would get from the development." Hilda shook her head. "Can you imagine the disruption, the building noise, the pesticides from a golf course, not to mention taking away Dot's water supply? What a nightmare."

"Indeed," Brianna said slowly, her mind turning this new information over. "I hadn't heard about the development, only about the water issues. I still can't imagine Dot being pushed to murder over it, though."

"Oh, neither can I, dear." Hilda stopped her darning to reach for Brianna's hand. She gripped it with an earnest look in her eyes, and Brianna felt hope squeeze into her heart. "Your aunt is a kind soul. I can't believe it, either."

Brianna said goodbye to Hilda a minute later and stood, intending to speak with the mysterious Connor Pearce. When she scanned the room, he was gone. Brianna wrinkled her nose. How was she supposed to track down the elusive man now, besides hang out in the Bumblebee's dining room every mealtime? She would have to try again tomorrow because the cheese club's field trip was tonight. Magnus had emailed her this morning to remind her that the visit was still on, despite the Montague's loss and the death of Susan, a long-time member of the Gourmand Society. Magnus had blathered on about how keeping the Society running was a tribute to Susan's memory, but Brianna suspected that Magnus couldn't bear to disrupt his beloved cheese club.

She would have given the trip a hard pass, despite her interest in the water buffalo and their role in producing mozzarella, but she couldn't give up another chance to scout around the area of Susan's murder under the guise of a legitimate reason for being there. Devon couldn't possibly fault her for that.

Brianna stopped beside her bicycle leaning against the Bumblebee's wooden siding and pulled out her phone. When Macy answered, Brianna sighed in relief.

"I'm glad I caught you," Brianna said. "Did you hear the news? Susan DeVries died from a water buffalo stampede, but I'm certain it wasn't an accident."

"What? Wait, do you think it has a connection to Owen's death?" Macy was quick on the uptake, and Brianna was glad she'd called.

"Yes, since I found evidence at the scene. I'll fill you

in with more details later, but since Susan is no longer a suspect, we're still looking at Tansy and Jay Montague, Shaun Bartley, Esmerelda Alonso, and the new guy in town. His name's Connor Pearce, and Susan pointed fingers at him when I spoke to her. I thought she was trying to deflect attention off herself, but now I wonder if there's more to her story than I first thought. Anyway, he's worth checking out, and I'll track him down soon, but my money is on Shaun."

"Don't wait too long to talk to Connor," Macy warned. "If he's a visitor, he could leave at any time."

"Hilda said he's here for a little longer, hiking and whatnot. But yes, I'll find him tomorrow."

"Oh, I wanted to tell you. I was chatting with Patty at preschool pickup—her little daughter Tamara is such a cutie pie—and she's a Mountie, too, so I did a little extra chatting. I got Owen's time of death, which was approximately nine that morning. Also, turns out Owen's autopsy report showed sleeping pills in his system. Not enough to kill him—the pitchfork definitely did that—but enough to make him woozy, for sure. According to Tansy, Owen often took them for his insomnia. It probably gave the killer an edge, anyway."

"Hmm." Brianna wasn't sure what to make of that information, but she tucked it away just in case. "Good sleuthing."

"Stay safe. I'll dig around for info about Connor, see what I can find out."

Brianna signed off and tucked her phone in her pocket with a lighter heart. She might not have the support of Devon and the authorities, but she could count on Macy.

Chapter 17

There wasn't much Brianna could do to find Connor until tomorrow, and she wasn't due at the Gourmand Society field trip until the evening. She didn't want to go to the café with potential killer Shaun there, and she didn't feel like retreating to her float home quite yet, despite the paperwork that desperately needed doing. How could she pass her afternoon?

She had a list of things to buy at the hardware store for her café renovations, but she wasn't in the mood for productivity. A brilliant notion snuck into her head, fueled by her talk with the incarcerated Dot the other day. What if she went sailing?

It was too inspired of an idea to pass up. Besides, she reasoned to herself, she could take an action selfie to put on her café's website in the 'about' section. Technically, she'd be working. Brianna swung her leg over her bike and pedaled in the direction of the marina.

After a warm ride through Snuggler's Cove, Brianna locked up her bicycle and strode with sure steps toward the racks where the smaller boats were stored on the far dock. Each was secured in its wooden rack with a hinged bar across the front and a combination lock holding it in place. Brianna held Dot's lock in her hand. Its blue numbers were so familiar, but Brianna's heart stuttered. Did she remember the combination?

She half-closed her eyes and let her fingers move on

their own. With slow but sure motions, her hands found the numbers that her brain had forgotten. After the third number, she yanked downward, and a satisfying thud freed the lock.

Mentally patting herself on her back, Brianna flipped the bar out of the way and tugged at the boat. It was flipped so its hull faced the sky, and she heaved it along the worn wood of the rack with a grating sound.

It was heavier than Brianna remembered, and she paused her motions to think. Could she do this by herself? Maybe taking the Guster out was a terrible idea. But if she didn't do it on her own, who knew when Dot would be around to sail with her? Brianna was even more convinced that her aunt was innocent, after Susan's suspicious death which must have been connected to Owen's, but Dot hadn't been released yet.

"Don't do that by yourself," a gruff voice said from behind Brianna. She whirled around to face Magnus Pickleton, who shook his head at her. "It's too heavy for one. Here, I'll take the other side."

Not one to deny an offer of help, Brianna said her thanks and gripped one side of the small boat. Magnus seized the other side and, with a huff, the two of them pulled the dinghy off the rack and flipped it to splash into the water. Magnus tied the painter to a cleat on the dock with an expert hand.

"I forgot, you own the marina, don't you?" Brianna said to him. "Thanks for the help."

"You're not going out on your own in that, are you?" Magnus frowned at her, a piece of lettuce wiggling in the depths of his beard. "What's your sailing experience like?

A city girl like you, you won't know how to navigate these waters."

Brianna drew herself up. "I've sailed here plenty," she said. "This is where I learned, in fact. My aunt Dot Dubois taught me."

"I suppose she's an old hand at the tiller," Magnus acknowledged with a reluctant tilt of his head. "Where's your lifejacket?"

He pulled the straps of a faded lifejacket that rested on a small shelf below the Guster's rack. With a squawk, a pigeon burst out from under the jacket and flew past Magnus in a whirlwind of flapping wings. He released an undignified shriek, and a startled Brianna put her hand over her mouth to cover her grin.

"There it is," she said. "Thanks for digging it out, and for help with the boat. Looks like I'm ready to go."

With a glower at the pigeon in the sky, Magnus stumped down the dock toward the marina's office. Brianna released her chuckle once he was out of earshot then shook out feathers from the lifejacket and slipped it on. The zipper was stiff from weather and lack of use, but when it was zipped up, the slight constriction centered Brianna and brought her back to summers of her youth.

She took a deep breath of sea air and climbed with unsteady legs into the bobbing boat then untied the painter from the dock. Her hands fumbled at the halyard for a moment, then a light gust of wind filled the sail. With a jolt, the boat started to move, and Brianna adjusted her position from muscle memory. The Guster sailed away from the dock and into the bay, cutting through the calm water like a knife through butter.

Brianna beamed, her mouth open with joy. She'd forgotten how freeing sailing was, how powerful it felt to harness the wind in a triangle of fabric, relying on nothing except the natural world around her. When the wind blew, she moved. When it didn't, she stopped. Compared to the mysteries surrounding the recent murders on the island, this was blissfully simple.

She pulled out her phone with difficulty using her free hand, the other one on the tiller, and raised it to grab a photo of herself with curls flying in the wind and a wide smile of bright-eyed joy on her face. It would do nicely for the website of an island-based café.

The thought of the murders brought her mind back to Dot, but Brianna only allowed herself a moment of sadness before she pushed it away. Hopefully, she and Dot could sail these waters together soon. But for today, Brianna was here, and that was enough.

The sun was only halfway down the blue sky lined with fleecy, cotton-ball clouds when Brianna pulled up to Susan's barn once more. This time, her bike joined five other vehicles parked along the barn's edge. She recognized most of them as owned by members of the cheese club.

The Gourmand Society stood just inside the water buffalo enclosure, their faces solemn and the air quiet.

Jay Montague stood a little apart from the others, his own expression closed and his eyes gazing at the black animals in the pond. When Brianna joined them, Hilda murmured a hello and Esme nodded at her. Magnus cleared his throat.

"This is a sad day for us all." He gazed around impassively at the little group. No one denied his words. "We have lost a valued fellow of our Society. Susan was a founding member, and she contributed much to her role as member-at-large. Let's not forget the excellent history of cheese that she often regaled us with. Susan will be greatly missed."

Hilda coughed with a pointed look at Jay, and Magnus spoke again.

"Of course, we must mention the loss of another important figure in the cheese industry of Driftwood Island. Owen Montague was a pillar of the community and a leader of the dairy industry with an entrepreneurial spirit." He turned to Jay. "Our condolences to you and your mother, Jay."

"Thanks," the younger man muttered, not meeting anyone's eye. "Are you ready to see the animals?"

They followed Jay across the field. Brianna was glad she'd brought boots, because the ground grew marshier the closer they drew to the pond. Hilda wandered next to Brianna as they trailed the group.

"I wanted to tell you," Hilda said quietly to Brianna, "I was feeding Susan's cat before we arrived—poor thing doesn't know where Susan is, but it still needs to eat, doesn't it—and I happened upon some strange papers on Susan's desk, quite by accident."

Brianna doubted that very much. Hilda seemed like an incurable gossip, and the lure of information about the dead woman had likely been too difficult to resist.

"Oh?" she said with real interest. Susan wasn't a suspect anymore, but her murder pointed to her involvement in whatever was going on behind the scenes. If Hilda had found something of interest, Brianna wasn't going to pretend she didn't care. "What was it?"

"An email print-out," Hilda said quietly. "Susan was a Luddite and hated reading anything on a screen. I saw Owen Montague's name on the email, as well as Connor Pearce's. I couldn't make heads or tails out of the message, although the tone was rather abrupt. Very strange."

Brianna broke away from Hilda when Esme shot them a curious glance. The woman wearing a caftan of bright orange swirls and matching dangly earrings was still a suspect, and Brianna didn't want Esme to grow suspicious of her, just in case she decided that the new café owner was a loose end to tie up.

Jay clucked his tongue, his boots ankle deep in mud, and a small water buffalo meandered closer to him out of the pond. Its coarse, grayish black hair shone in the sun, and its tan-colored horns curled backward with a serious point at the end. The buffalo gazed at Jay with glossy black eyes as it approached.

Jay scratched the animal's head with real fondness, and the buffalo pushed against his side with her large forehead, avoiding hitting his body with her horns. Jay had slung the strap of a cattle prod over his shoulder, maybe because of the stampede that killed Susan, although it looked like he had no intention of using it.

"This is Laila," he said, a light in his eyes for the first time. "She's a year old, and the friendliest of the bunch. Once she breeds next year and calves, she'll be ready for milking like the rest of the herd. We have twenty lactating buffalos at the moment, plus a few young males and calves. Water buffalos will calve anytime, so there's always a few little guys running around."

Brianna stepped forward with a cautious eye on Laila. The animal glanced at her, and her ears flicked.

"I've tasted the cheese that's made from your buffalos' milk," she said to Jay with a nod at Laila. "What do you feed them to get the milk so creamy and flavorful?"

"It's mostly just the buffalo you taste," Jay said with a shrug. "They eat mainly grass, but we supplement with hay and some vegetable rejects from the grocery store."

"Aren't these beasts from the tropics, originally?" Esme said from the back of the group. "What do you do in the winter? It doesn't get that cold here, but freezing is freezing to an animal from the equator."

"They're pretty tough, but they live in the barn during the coldest months." Jay pointed at the structure behind them. "That's where the milking equipment is, too. I'll show you."

Jay patted Laila once more before leading the Gourmand Society to a wide barn door that opened to the pasture. Brianna glanced at Laila again, but the water buffalo had turned back to munch grass at her feet. The animals certainly didn't seem very dangerous, but she supposed that if they were frightened, a mad rush of the heavy beasts would trample anyone.

"Here's the milking parlor." Jay pointed at a clean stall with technical-looking equipment on the side. The end opened into a window to the pasture, and a trough provided a place for feed. "We milk each heifer here. To make the milk come faster, we feed them during milking, and we make sure the calves are within sight." Jay shrugged with a shy grin. "It was my idea. My dad thought it was stupid, but the animals seem to like the reminder of what the milk is for."

Jay struck Brianna as very invested in the water buffalo business, and that idea cemented itself in her mind the more Jay showed them around the barn and milking contraptions. It was a fascinating insight into water buffalo husbandry as well as Jay Montague's personality, and Brianna wondered how much Owen had liked the buffalo compared to his son's care and interest.

Esme's colorful clothing caught Brianna's eye, and she recalled her intention to speak with the other woman. Just because Hilda hadn't seen her buying a smoothie the morning of Owen's murder didn't mean that she was innocent. While Quentin asked technical questions about calving and milk production, Brianna touched Esme's elbow and invited her with a nod to speak at the back of the barn.

"Esme," Brianna began. She needed answers from the other woman, and it was time to start asking more direct questions. Whereas she'd been fearful of retaliation when confronting temperamental, muscly Shaun, flamboyant Esme felt like less of a threat, especially with the

Gourmand Society at Brianna's back. "Where were you last night?"

Chapter 18

Esme frowned, then her eyes widened in the dim light of the barn. "You mean where was I when poor Susan died? Oh, I wish I'd been here to stop her. What a gruesome way to go. I hope it was quick and that she didn't suffer much."

"I don't believe Susan's death was an accident," Brianna said bluntly. "In fact, I think it was connected to Owen Montague's murder. You had history with Owen, some secret that he was threatening to expose. It might have been enough motive to kill him. I'm still working out why you might target Susan."

Esme put her hand to her chest. "You think I killed them both?" she whispered, her shoulders shuddering. "You can't possibly think that."

"You have no one to confirm your whereabouts the morning of Owen's death," Brianna continued. Her eyes drilled into Esme's face, searching for the barest hint of deceit. So far, she'd found none, but she didn't know how skilled Esme was at subterfuge. "So, I ask again: where were you the night of Susan's death?"

"I wasn't even on the island last night," she hissed, her eyes bright with outrage. "I was visiting my sister on the mainland. And you want to know why I fought with Owen?" She looked away, her lip trembling. "Fine, I'll tell you. You never met him, but Owen Montague was a sexy man. Handsome, confident, willing to spend money. I approached him one day, and he turned me down. I was willing to overlook the slight, thinking he was a devoted family man, then I found out he was sleeping with Diana Bartley on the side." Her eyes flashed. "So, I threatened to review his milk business unfavorably. My word holds a lot of weight in the food world, and I know many top restaurants in the area buy cheese made from his milk." Esme's eyes dropped to her beringed fingers. "Maybe it was a little spiteful."

"Then what happened?" Brianna prompted when the silence lingered.

"Owen somehow found out that—" Esme swallowed, and her eyes darted around the barn to make sure no one was close enough to hear. "That I'd faked an email from chef Cecil Gagnon to Plate magazine, praising my critic abilities. If it ever came out that I'd fabricated that email, my career would be ruined. But I didn't kill Owen, I swear. I already felt bad for threatening his business. I had no intention of following through with my earlier threat."

Brianna let out her breath in a long sigh. Esme's words rang of truth, but she had to be sure.

"Can anyone confirm that you weren't on the island last night?" she asked.

"Quentin drove me to the ferry," she said with a haughty tilt of her head that covered her vulnerability with a veneer of pride after confessing her fraud and romantic failures. "Ask him."

Quentin was speaking with Hilda outside the barn at this point, but he broke off when Brianna approached him across the dirt parking area.

"Quentin," she said. "Did you drop off Esme at the ferry yesterday? Did she get on?"

"I did," he said without a flicker of eyes toward Esme, which convinced Brianna that he was telling the truth. They hadn't even communicated with a look before she asked her question. "She doesn't like paying for her car on the ferry, so she gets me to chauffer her in exchange for bringing back a bag of my favorite brand of coffee from the mainland."

Brianna hung her head, then turned back to Esme who was waiting with crossed arms.

"I'm sorry for accusing you," she said formally. "I hope you can understand my motives. My aunt is in custody, and I don't believe she's the culprit. I'm trying to figure out what actually happened so she can walk free."

Esme milked the moment for longer than Brianna wanted. She tried not to squirm.

"Apology accepted," the other woman said finally. Her eyes pierced Brianna with a gleam of curiosity. "But now you must tell me what's happening. I smell a mystery. If it has something to do with Susan's death, then I want to know. She might have been a vindictive cow, but she was one of us."

"What's going on?" Quentin said, his eyes flashing between Brianna and Esme behind his round glasses.

Brianna glanced at Esme who waved a languid hand toward her in invitation. Since Esme was exonerated, and none of the others had ever been suspects, Brianna told the whole saga to Quentin, who was quickly joined by Magnus and Hilda after Jay roared off in his pickup.

Quentin listened with intense eyebrows, and Hilda gasped in all the right places. Magnus's scowl deepened with every word Brianna spoke.

"Well," Magnus said after Brianna finished her tale. "It's Shaun Bartley, clear as day."

"A hot-tempered man like that, there's no knowing what he could do," Hilda agreed. "And it can't be Tansy, because I was chatting to her friend Grace, and she said Tansy visited with her last night, right at the time of Susan's death. Apparently, she died at nine thirty yesterday evening, according to Patty from the station. She gave me a ride at the car stop this morning."

"Very few men like sharing their woman," Esme said with a sage nod. "Shaun's your culprit, Brianna."

"I don't disagree, for Owen's death," Brianna said. "But what reason would Shaun have to kill Susan?"

"Cleaning up loose ends?" Quentin suggested. "Maybe Susan found out and confronted him."

"Ooo, that would be just like Susan," Hilda said. Her fingers twitched as if missing her darning needle. "Sticking her nose in where it doesn't fit, bless her soul."

"Maybe," Brianna said. "Shaun does fit the bill. And whoever attacked Owen could have easily grabbed Dot's pitchfork from where it was leaning against the shared fence. I could see someone angry snatching the first weapon they could find nearby. Okay, I'll poke around more for clues. Thanks for your help, everyone."

"Of course." Magnus drew himself up. "The Gourmand Society defends the cheese industry on Driftwood Island and protects its own."

"Even the nosy busybody members," Esme said.

Brianna rode home in the dusky light, too fired up to mind about the dimly lit woods and blank driveways she passed around Mt. Dashton. She stopped at Dot's house on the way and tossed in an armful of alfalfa for Zola. The goat stuck her head through the fence and butted Brianna's side.

"I'm sorry, Zola." Brianna scratched the animal's head. "You're missing Dot too, aren't you? I'm doing everything I can to bring her home, I promise."

Her heart twisted when she left the goat alone. The animal gazed at her pedaling away, and it wasn't until Brianna reached the road that Zola bent her head to her dinner. Brianna's jaw clenched, and she promised herself to press harder in her search for clues.

After quickly changing her clothes at home and dashing outside, Brianna clutched her tin of baking to her chest and surveyed the crowded dock. The float home inhabitants had taken over the wharf next to Brianna's home. She didn't recognize anyone.

Brianna straightened her shoulders and took a deep breath. She didn't know anyone yet. That was the point of her attending this wharf party, after all. An event like this never would have happened in her Vancouver condo. There, most people had gone out of their way to avoid contact. An event like this was one of the reasons she'd looked forward to moving to Driftwood Island. It just took a little courage to dive into her new life. But if she could confront a potential murderer and live to tell the tale, she could probably handle a party.

She walked down the gently shifting dock. The teenaged figure she'd met in front of her float home a couple of weeks ago disengaged from the crowd and eyed her tin with interest.

"New girl," Joel said. "You came bearing gifts. I heard you bake or something."

"Help yourself." Brianna opened the lid and offered the tin to Joel. Inside, mounds of golden-brown cheese puffs waited for Joel's quick fingers. He didn't make them wait for long.

"They're pretty good," he said through his mouthful. "What are they?"

"Gruyère gougères." Brianna hid a grin as Joel selected another. "Say that five times fast. Honest opinions are appreciated. I'm trying to decide whether to serve them in my new café, and you're my guinea pig."

Joel nibbled at his next gougère with buck teeth, and Brianna laughed.

"Joel!" A kindly looking woman in a knee-length yellow sundress with red curls to rival Brianna's own approached and shook her head. "Did you corner this poor lady? My son will eat the whole tin if you let him. I'd say he grew up in a barn if I didn't know better. I did my best, I swear."

"Mom, this is Brianna from the blue house," Joel said after he swallowed, an unrepentant grin on his face. He'd clearly heard his mother's admonishments before.

"Brianna West." Brianna stuck out her hand and the other woman shook it firmly.

"Alicia Marley, from the log cabin." She pointed at the wooden home with plants and spinning whirligigs on the rooftop patio.

"Alicia Marley the realtor?" Brianna recognized the name from her house purchase, but Dot had handled all in-person interactions. It was nice to finally put a face to the name.

"One and the same." Alicia beamed then turned to her son. "Joel, will you get us two glasses of wine? Your dad just opened a bottle from Orca Vineyard, and we should introduce our new neighbor to the bounties of our island."

"Introduce her to your lush club, you mean?" Joel shot his mother a cheeky grin. She swatted him and he darted off.

"Teenagers." Alicia sighed. "Can't live with them, can't live without them. So, Brianna, how are you settling in? Enjoying your float home so far? It's an unusual lifestyle, but you'll find its proponents can be borderline fanatical." She chuckled and glanced at the crowd.

"I can see why," Brianna said. "My home is snug and compact but has everything I need. And no yard to maintain is a definite plus. I have enough going on with the café."

"Yes, tell me more about your café. When is it opening?"

Alicia eyed the baking tin, and Brianna thrust it toward her in offering.

"The grand opening of the Golden Moon is a week Saturday," she said proudly. "Please, try a gruyère gougère. Everything in the café will have cheese as an ingredient."

"What a delicious idea." Alicia popped a gougère into her mouth and chewed. A look of rapture crossed her face. "Mmm. I can see why Joel was gorging himself. Mind you, he'll eat anything that's in front of him, but these are really good."

A balding man with glasses and twinkling eyes walked up to them with two glasses of deep red wine in hand. He passed one to each of the women and wrapped an arm around Alicia's waist.

"My husband, Cliff," Alicia explained. "Cliff, meet Brianna. She's opening a café where everything will have cheese in it, doesn't that sound fun?"

"My kind of place," Cliff said. "Nice to meet you, Brianna. Try this merlot and tell us what cheese you think it would pair best with. Too bad the vintner is a nasty piece of work because his wines are divine."

Brianna closed her eyes and sniffed the wine, which released a faint scent of plum and tea. She took a delicate sip and let the flavors coat her tongue. After her swallow, the aftertaste lingered in her mouth.

"A herbed goat chèvre," she said at last. "On rye crackers."

Cliff nodded with an appreciative gleam. "That makes me hungry. Who's ready for burgers?"

Brianna followed the two after Alicia drew her

forward by the elbow to meet other float home inhabitants. The scent of cooking meat filled the air, and happy chatter included her in its midst. Brianna took a deep breath, but it was a breath of relief and happiness, not nerves. It was early days, but she might have finally found a place to belong.

Chapter 19

The party had been a pleasant distraction, but once Brianna entered her float home under the starlit sky, it was ages before she felt settled enough to sleep. Evidence, rumors, and facts swirled in her mind without cease.

She was relieved to cross Esme Alonso off her suspect list. She hadn't liked thinking that the flamboyant, outspoken woman was a cold-blooded killer, and she doubted that the Gourmand Society would be able to sustain another loss within its little community.

Shaun Bartley and Connor Pearce were high on her list now. She planned to search for Connor at lunchtime at the B&B. Shaun should be at her café in the morning, finishing up the counter. If she were careful by keeping the doors open for a quick getaway, then she could cautiously ask more questions of the carpenter. His opinion of Susan, for instance, and his whereabouts the night of her death.

Brianna fell asleep to the thought of questioning Shaun in her yellow dining room of the Golden Moon. In her dreams, a huge moon shone an illuminating light on the culprit, whose turned-away face was hidden from Brianna's sight.

The next morning, Brianna woke early with her brain revving up as soon as her eyes opened. She didn't have a chance at falling back asleep, not now, so she rolled out of her low bed and proceeded to start her day. Early morning was an excellent time to get some work done on the cafe while Shaun was absent, and she could rehearse what she planned to say to him while she baked and painted.

That morning in her cheery café kitchen, she planned to bake asiago buns, fluffy bread rolls that resembled cinnamon rolls but with cheese and bacon bits instead of sugar and raisins. She'd prepped a dough the day before and had left it in the fridge to slowly rise. While it warmed up, she would grate cheese, fry and chop bacon, and melt butter in preparation.

Brianna smiled at her freshly painted sign and awning gleaming in the warmth of a morning sun, then she parked in the alley between the café and the yarn shop which was quiet at this hour. She unlocked the side door that led to the kitchen and hung her purse on a hook by the door, then she pulled an apron over her head. As she was tying a bow behind her back with the apron strings, her eyes glanced at the counter. Her fingers froze.

A large ball of white cheese sat on the butcher block counter. Stabbed into the center of the creamy sphere, standing straight upright, was the largest, sharpest carving knife Brianna owned.

Brianna's heart thudded in her ears. Who had set up this threatening tableau? It was a message, of that Brianna had no doubt. Someone knew she was hunting for answers and wanted her to stop.

Was the person still here? Brianna held her breath and listened for sounds, but the kitchen and café beyond held an empty silence. She tiptoed to the open doorway between kitchen and dining area and peeked her head over the threshold, but the golden yellow space was unoccupied. Brianna crept to the bathroom, but it, too was empty.

She returned to the kitchen and stared at the cheese. It was a good-sized ball of mozzarella, if her eyes and nose were to be believed. She touched the firm white surface. It was still cool, which meant that it hadn't been out of the fridge for long. The murderer had been in her kitchen within the last hour.

Brianna gripped the counter to steady herself. How had the killer entered? She raced to the front door and turned the handle easily. Had Shaun left it open last night by accident? Or had the carpenter set up the cheese and knife because he was the murderer?

Brianna returned to the kitchen with shaky legs and carefully tugged the knife out of her beautiful cheese by the portion of blade that was still exposed. She avoided touching the handle. When she dropped it on the counter, it clanged loudly enough for her to jump in fright.

"Get a grip," she whispered to herself, a hand on her thundering heart.

She wrapped the cheese in its carelessly discarded package on a nearby counter and tucked it back in the fridge. Then she leaned her elbows on the butcher block and hung her head between them to collect herself.

Although the threat was a shock, it was actually a good sign. It meant that Brianna was getting close to answers, close enough that the murderer felt threatened by her. She wished with every fiber of her being that she had more physical evidence to present to Devon and the Major Crime Unit, but she had nothing but conjecture and theories. Good ones, but Devon had made it clear that they weren't welcome without solid proof.

But she had a knife touched by the murderer, or at least an accomplice. After Brianna's heart resumed to almost normal speed, she raised her head. She needed to check for fingerprints. If the killer were clever, they'd have worn gloves, but she had to find out.

She opened a cupboard and took out a container of cornstarch, the finest powder in her kitchen. She sprinkled a tiny bit of cornstarch on a makeup brush she dug out of the bottom of her purse, shook it to remove excess particles, and carefully ran the brush over the knife's handle in circular motions.

When no fingerprints appeared on the handle, she flipped it over and dusted the other side. No marks appeared. The stabber must have worn gloves. Brianna's heart sank, but her jaw tightened. This threat hadn't deterred her. If anything, it fueled her determination to find the truth.

But she couldn't do anything about her quest right that moment, so with gritted teeth, she pulled open the fridge and took out her proofing dough. By the time the front door slammed open and a whistling announced Shaun's arrival, Brianna had a rack full of cooling cheese and bacon buns and a spine of steel, ready for her confrontation.

"Hi, Brianna," Shaun greeted her when she entered the dining area. "Something smells good, as usual."

"Asiago and bacon buns this morning," she said with false cheer. She walked to the door and propped it open with an old brick. "I'll leave a few out for you for your break. It's such a gorgeous day, I figure you could use the fresh air."

"Good idea." Shaun dropped his work bag and stretched his arms. "That counter will be done today, I promise. Stain and glass and everything."

"Good news."

Brianna walked to the kitchen and turned to lean against the doorway. She liked having the kitchen exit at her back. Shaun's shirt was tight against his biceps, and she swallowed nervously. Running was the only option if things went south. She would have to be smart about her questions to avoid a situation.

"Did you hear about Susan DeVries's death Thursday night?" she asked.

"Terrible tragedy." Shaun didn't look at her while he wrenched open a tin of stain with his hammer. "I didn't know water buffalo were so vicious. You'd better believe I warned Jack to stay away from the DeVries property. He's not old enough to wander the island on his own yet, but those days are fast approaching, and he needs to know where to avoid."

"Good thinking." Brianna tapped her fingers on her thigh. How could she pry further? "To think I was at home, tucked up on the couch, at the exact same time that Susan was breathing her last. Where were you?"

"Out," he said vaguely. "Not thinking about Susan DeVries, that's for sure."

"Were you in my kitchen earlier this morning?" Brianna blurted out. She needed answers, and Shaun wasn't providing them as quickly as she wanted. Pushing him was a risk, but she needed to solve this case before the murderer decided to stick a knife in her instead of in her cheese. She pushed away from the door and braced herself to run.

"No," Shaun said slowly. He looked at her with a frown. "Why?"

Brianna opened her mouth to reply—with what, she wasn't yet sure—when motion caught her eye. Macy was silhouetted in the open doorway.

It's not Shaun, she mouthed. *Stop.*

Chapter 20

Brianna melted against the doorframe of the Golden Moon again and looked at the waiting Shaun.

"No reason," she said. "I just hoped you hadn't come looking for a snack and I'd forgot to leave one out. I'd hate for you to go hungry on the job."

Shaun grinned and picked up a paintbrush. "Not likely at this gig."

Brianna left Shaun at the counter and walked outside to speak with Macy. Once they were around the corner and out of earshot, Macy whirled around.

"You looked like you were about to accuse Shaun of murder. Did you accuse him? What did he say?"

"It's fine," Brianna assured her, although a shiver passed down her spine at her close call. She would have ruined her relationship with her carpenter over nothing, and it was too close to opening day to mess that up. "I asked him some questions, but I didn't accuse him of anything. What did you find out? How did you know he's not our guy?"

Macy leaned against the wall with a sigh, unmindful of the dusty brick touching her floral blouse. "Magnus told me Shaun was working for him at the marina Thursday night until late, past the time the coroner said Susan died. Magnus figured Shaun was happy to keep working because of troubles at home. He and Diana are on the rocks, apparently. Magnus isn't the biggest gossip, but he still let that tidbit slip."

"Trouble in paradise." Brianna put her hands behind her head while she thought. "I really wondered if it was Shaun. You know, I found a ball of mozzarella stabbed through with a knife in my kitchen this morning. I thought it might have been Shaun warning me off the case."

Macy stared with a slack jaw. "You're getting threats now?" she whispered. "That's bad. We need to figure this out, and fast. What do we know?"

"Shaun's not our killer, not of Susan, anyway. Looks like he found out about the affair, though. Could the murders be unrelated after all?"

"Except that Shaun was dropping his son Jack off at school the morning of Owen's murder," Macy said. "I heard it through one of the preschool parents. He's not the killer. And Oaklyn saw Jay at the pizza joint in town on the night of Susan's death—they were both there all evening." Macy scowled. "He's at least five years older than her. She'd better not be batting her eyelashes at him."

"So, our best guess now is this Connor Pearce guy." Brianna stared at Macy, who wriggled with impatience. "Do you have something to say?"

"Yes," she said. "A little late-night searching will turn up wonders on the Internet. I found Connor's date of birth on a social media site—guess he's not that savvy about his privacy—then I used the criminal record check service we use when hiring at the preschool. Turns out he's been arrested for break and enter, drug possession, and assault."

"It doesn't look good. You think he's our guy, that he has something to do with Owen's shady past?"

Macy crossed her arms. "All I'm saying is that he's a prime suspect. If Susan found out about Owen's past, maybe Connor was cleaning up."

"I think we need to talk to Connor," Brianna said. "Right now."

"I have the afternoon off." Macy pointed at her car, illegally parked across the entrance of Brianna's alley again. "Hop in."

Brianna's stomach rumbled, and she ran into the café's kitchen to grab her purse and a few cheese buns for her and Macy to nibble on the way over to the Bumblebee. It wasn't far to the B&B, and Brianna filled Macy in on more details of her findings about Esme Alonso at the Gourmand Society's field trip. When Macy pulled into the parking lot at their destination, she stopped the car and turned to Brianna with a serious expression.

"What's the plan?" she said. "We want to talk to a potential murderer here. One with a shady history and possible link to Owen's strange past. Money is clearly involved, given the Montague's expensive house. Selling milk doesn't pay that well. What are we talking about, here? Mafia or something?"

Brianna bit her lip. "I don't know. Let's try to speak with him in a public place. Hopefully he's in the dining room and we can corner him there. Surely, he wouldn't do anything with witnesses."

"Who knows, with these types," Macy muttered. She pushed her keys into her purse and opened the car door.

"Okay, I'm ready to swim with the sharks. Keep an eye out for Oaklyn if I die, won't you?"

"Don't say that," Brianna chided, although her stomach roiled with nerves. "We're not accusing him of anything. We're just going to talk to him casually."

Macy gave her a disbelieving look but didn't comment further. Brianna followed her out of the car and up the porch steps of the B&B. She supposed she deserved that look. She had almost accused Shaun Bartley that very day.

But while Shaun was a hot-tempered carpenter, Connor Pearce was an unknown quantity. Was he really the cold-blooded killer of Owen Montague and Susan DeVries? What had Owen been embroiled in, and was Connor part of some larger organization sent to silence the water buffalo farmer? Brianna squared her shoulders and marched up the stairs. That was why she was here, to get answers to these nebulous questions. Suspicion might be falling off Dot—she hoped—but someone had threatened Brianna herself, and she needed answers.

Hilda wasn't in the dining room today when they entered. A cheery woman who looked like Hilda's daughter greeted them at the entrance.

"Table for two?" she said comfortably.

Brianna shook her head, and Macy tugged at her elbow.

"There he is," she whispered.

"We're joining a friend," Brianna said to the greeter. "I see him now."

The woman watched them with curiosity as they approached Connor, who sat in a corner at a small table covered with a white tablecloth with embroidered bees along the edge in yellow and black.

"Why did you say friend?" Macy hissed at her. "Now everyone will think you know him, which is awkward if he really is mafioso or whatever. You know how Hilda Button talks, and her daughter isn't much better."

Brianna winced. She'd blurted out the sort of excuse she would have done in the city, but that didn't fly in a small town like Snuggler's Cove. Hopefully she could explain to Hilda later.

She didn't have time to answer Macy before they arrived at Connor's table. Macy let Brianna approach first, despite Brianna's glare at her friend, leaving her alone to speak. She had no idea what to say, so she decided to get to the point.

"Hello, Connor Pearce?" she said with an attempt at a friendly, competent tone. "I'm Brianna West. Could I talk to you for a minute?"

Connor glanced up from his book on hiking in the area and stared at her with hazel eyes for a long moment. His expression was blank and revealed nothing of his thoughts. He was younger than she'd previously assumed, maybe a few years older than her, but weathered in a way her middle-class city life hadn't exposed her to. Brianna squirmed under his assessment and wondered what he thought he saw.

"Sure," he said finally. His eyes flicked to Macy, who was hanging back. "Your friend, too, I'm guessing."

"Thanks." Brianna breathed a sigh of relief and sank into the seat opposite Connor against the wall. Macy dragged a chair close to Brianna and perched on the edge.

"Macy Jones," she said quietly when Connor looked at her.

He nodded and took a bite of his sandwich. His eyes gazed at Brianna, waiting for her to say something.

Was there any point in faking small talk with Connor? Brianna wanted this conversation to be over before it started. Connor's hazel eyes saw too much, and she was starting to sweat. If he really were the killer, they were drawing far too much attention to themselves.

"I'll be brief, since I'm interrupting your lunch," she said, happy that her voice wasn't trembling. "Two people have been murdered in town, and someone has pointed their finger in your direction. I would love to hear your alibis and your side of the story."

Macy gaped at her. Brianna clenched her hands together until the fingers grew white and sore. She should have let Macy do the talking. What would Connor possibly say to her terrible accusation?

A brief expression of bitter disappointment clouded Connor's face before he looked at his sandwich with a mask of indifference firmly pasted on.

"I didn't kill anyone," he said flatly. "Tell me when these murders happened, and I'll tell you what I was doing."

"Where were you Thursday evening?"

"In my room at the Bumblebee, from after dinner onward."

"So, no one can corroborate that?" Brianna held her breath.

Connor shrugged. "A staff member might have seen

me, but I'm a visitor here. No one knows me or cares what I do."

The words were steeped with a bitterness that surprised Brianna. She swallowed and continued her relentless questions, frustrated that she had to ask them, but still not convinced that Connor wasn't the killer.

"The first murder was of Owen Montague. Do you have a connection with him?"

Connor's face was thunderous. "No," he spat out. "I have nothing to do with Owen."

"You were seen arguing with him last week," Macy said after a glance at Brianna. "What were you arguing about?"

"Wow." Connor sat back and stared at the two of them. "You think I killed Owen Montague. Why doesn't that surprise me? I guess I'm an easy target. It couldn't possibly be someone from this little island paradise. Everyone here is perfect. It must be the outsider, the shabby guy that no one knows. He's the best one to take the fall."

Brianna's stomach twinged with guilt. He wasn't entirely wrong that some of their assumptions had come from observing Connor's looks and demeanor. The argument with Owen was still suspicious, though, and Brianna set aside her feelings to probe further.

"Owen's murder took place last Sunday morning. What were you doing then?"

"I was visiting my aunt. You might know her? Dot Dubois."

Brianna stared at the man across from her then exchanged an incredulous glance with Macy. Dot had only one brother—Brianna's father—and Brianna and her own brother were Dot's only niece and nephew. Why would Connor say he was related to Dot? Was it perhaps an honorary title, some old family friend that Brianna had never heard of?

"Dot Dubois is your aunt," Brianna said, her voice thick with skepticism. Who was he to claim kinship with her beloved aunt? She wanted to reach across and shake the truth out of Connor but managed to rein herself in. "And you were visiting with her during the murder."

Connor nodded, his eyes not leaving her face. Brianna's breath caught. Just before she'd found Owen's body, Brianna had arrived at Dot's house and surprised her aunt traipsing out of the woods, covered in mud. She hadn't satisfactorily said where she'd been. Had she been with Connor? Was Dot's confession correct, or perhaps she was covering up for Connor after witnessing his murderous antics? What was their true connection, and why would Dot take the fall? Was Connor threatening her with something?

"You know Dot is in a correctional facility right now, awaiting trial," Brianna told Connor. "She confessed to the first murder, but I'm certain she didn't do it. Maybe she was covering up for someone else."

Brianna ignored Macy's warning kick and watched Connor's face carefully. His expression clouded over, and he pushed his sandwich away with a queasy look.

"How do you know she wasn't the killer?" he said, although his voice lacked conviction.

"Because I know her," Brianna said with heat. "She's my aunt, too."

Connor stared at her. His eyes raked over her face as if searching for something, and his lips parted in astonishment.

"Something doesn't add up," Macy said. "Connor, do have anything else you can tell us? We're desperately trying to get Dot out of custody for a crime we're sure she didn't commit. If you care about her at all, please tell us anything you know about the murders."

Macy made it sound like they weren't accusing Connor, which was clever but probably too little, too late after Brianna's pointed probing. Brianna bit her lip and waited for Connor's answer. He stared at her again.

"No," he said finally. "I don't know who killed those two people, but it wasn't me. That's all I can tell you."

Macy stood and pulled at Brianna's elbow until she followed. "Thanks for your time," she said to Connor. "We'll leave you to the rest of your lunch."

Brianna stumbled after Macy but glanced back once at Connor. He stared at his sandwich as if it contained answers he sought.

Chapter 21

Macy propelled Brianna with iron fingers until they reached the car.

"What on earth was that?" she shrieked. She took a deep breath and continued more calmly. "You weren't exactly subtle, considering we were talking to *a potential murderer*. What were you thinking?"

"I was thinking we needed answers," Brianna said defensively.

Her phone rang, sparing her from explaining further to an irate Macy. She didn't recognize the number and answered cautiously.

"Hello?"

"Brianna West?" a familiar voice answered. "This is Corporal Devon Moore. We have your aunt Dot Dubois. New evidence came to light, and the judge agreed that her confession wasn't enough to hold her at the corrections facility given the new information. She's been released and transferred back to our detachment, and she could use a ride home."

Brianna's heart swelled in her chest, and she forgot all about her concerns over Connor, Owen's history, the stabbed cheese, all of it. Dot was free!

"I'll be right there," she gasped.

Macy must have overheard Devon's words, because she was already in the car and turning the key.

"Get in, get in," she screeched. "And while we're

there, we'll talk to the Mounties about Connor. Their detectives need to nab him for questioning before the next ferry leaves, because you know he'll be on it."

Brianna sank into the passenger's seat, pushing aside a takeout container on the floor with her foot. A white baby shoe dangled on the rearview mirror, its leather cracked from age and sun exposure. It must have been worn by the now-teenaged Oaklyn many years ago.

Brianna twisted her fingers together while Macy careened around corners and sped down side streets toward the police station. Dot was free at last. Now, if the Mounties arrested Connor to interview him—assuming he was the murderer—then Brianna's quest would be complete. No more killing, no more locked-up Dot, no more threatening knives stabbed into her cheeses. All this could be over.

Macy turned into the city hall parking lot and jolted over a speedbump. As soon as the car stopped, Brianna leaped out and raced to the station door. Inside, she glanced around wildly until she spotted her aunt on a chair in the waiting area.

"Dot!" she cried and flung herself at her aunt. Dot stood and held her arms open for her niece with a wide smile. She looked tired and worn without makeup and much sleep, and she smelled of institutional antiseptic instead of her usual floral scent, but her arms were strong as they gripped Brianna tightly.

"You're a sight for sore eyes," she said with a light laugh. "Come on, let's get out of here before they change their minds."

Brianna wrapped her arm around Dot's shoulders and

drew her out the door. Macy was waiting for them at the car, beaming.

"Welcome back, Dot," she said. "You were missed."

Dot sighed happily and allowed Brianna to settle her in the front passenger's seat of Macy's hatchback.

"It wasn't the most comfortable stay," she said. "I'm glad to be home."

Brianna slid into the backseat and leaned forward to speak with her aunt while Macy turned her body to face them.

"Dot," Macy said, "Why did they let you go after your confession? And why did you confess if you didn't do it?"

Brianna jolted in surprise. Of course, those were the obvious questions to ask. She'd been so happy to see Dot that all thoughts of the mystery she was unwinding had fled her mind. Dot sighed again, although this time it wasn't a happy sound.

"Someone came forward, saying that they were with me Sunday morning, so I couldn't have been at the scene of the crime when Owen died." She scowled. "According to the forensics timeline, anyway."

"Well, that's good news," Brianna said. She still didn't understand Dot's role in all this. "But why did you confess in the first place? Who were you protecting?"

Dot shook her head and looked out the side window away from the other two.

"It doesn't matter," she said tightly. "Don't worry about it."

"Brianna has to worry about it," Macy said with heat. "Because she's been investigating the murders, and now the killer sent her a warning to back off. She'll be next if we don't figure this out, and the authorities aren't solving it with any great rush. But we think we know who did it, and we're just about to tell the police our suspicions."

Dot stared at Macy with fear in her eyes. "Who do you think killed Owen Montague?" she whispered.

"And Susan DeVries," Brianna added. Dot's eyes snapped to her face. "We're pretty sure it's Connor Pearce, the visitor who's staying at the Bumblebee. You know," she added, "your *nephew*."

Blood drained from Dot's face, and it grew as pale as buffalo milk.

"No," she whispered. "No, no, no. What evidence do you have against him?"

"Nothing concrete yet," Brianna admitted. "But enough suspicion that the police should sit up and take note."

"Please don't accuse Connor," Dot begged, her eyes filling with tears. "Please. Not without solid evidence. He deserves better than that."

Brianna glanced at Macy, who looked as flummoxed as she felt. Why was Dot protecting this man? What was he to her?

"It would really help me understand if you told me why you confessed to the murder," Brianna said to Dot. "What's going on here? Why is he calling you his aunt?"

Dot shook her head with jerky motions so that tears flew out of her eyes in wide arcs, but she only stared at Brianna without a word. Brianna sighed and slumped back in her seat, mulling over her options.

"Hilda Button," she said at last. "She found papers in

Susan's house that looked suspicious. Let's get her to let us in, and we can find our evidence, one way or another."

"We'd better be quick," Macy warned. "The ferry leaves at five o'clock. We need to have enough to arrest Connor before then, assuming he's the culprit."

Dot passed a shaking hand over her eyes. Brianna frowned at the back of her aunt's head but didn't say anything else. Gathering evidence wasn't a bad plan, in any event. Devon had made it clear that he didn't want to hear more rumors or conjectures, not without solid proof to back them up. Hopefully, something in Susan's papers would give her the evidence she needed to bolster her claims.

"Where would Hilda be on a Saturday afternoon?" Brianna wondered aloud.

"Mirror Mirror," Macy and Dot said together. Macy laughed, and Dot gave a weak chuckle.

"She's always at the hair salon on Saturday afternoons," Dot explained. "She gets her weekly blowout and gossip fix."

"To Mirror Mirror it is," Macy said, and she backed out of the parking spot and pulled onto the road.

They dropped a tired Dot at her house, then turned around and went back to Snuggler's Cove. It wasn't far to the salon, and Brianna stepped out of the car as soon as Macy pulled up to the curb in front of Mirror Mirror. Sure enough, Hilda Button was at the counter paying for her hair appointment and chatting with the proprietor.

"Brianna," Hilda said with a cheery wave. "Good to see you. I just finished." She patted her white curls. "What do you think?"

"Lovely." Brianna walked closer so she could speak quietly to the elderly woman. "I have a favor to ask. Could you take me to Susan's house to look at those odd papers you found? I'm trying to dig into who killed her, and I think those papers hold the key."

"Oh!" Hilda's eyes grew as round as her last name. "Of course. If I can help clear up this mystery of poor Susan's death, I'd be happy to. I need to feed Petunia again, anyway." She patted her purse then shuffled toward the door. "I'll need a ride, though. I usually use the car stop."

"Of course we can give you a ride," Macy said.

"Thanks so much for your help. By the way, what's the car stop?" asked Brianna.

"No buses on Driftwood Island," Macy explained. "So instead of bus stops, we have car stops. Sanctioned hitchhiking, basically. If you see someone waiting there, you can offer a ride."

"It's quite handy," Hilda said as she tottered slowly toward Macy's hatchback. "I don't drive anymore—luckily my granddaughter's preschool is so close to home, we walk every morning—and with the car stop, I can visit with everyone who picks me up. Oh, the stories I hear! It's quite marvelous."

Brianna twisted her fingers with impatience at Hilda's slow pace. Once she'd settled the elderly woman into the front passenger's seat, Brianna closed the door and stared imploringly at Macy, who chuckled.

"Don't ask Hilda to do anything fast," she whispered. "She'll be the first one to tell you she earned her right to take things her speed."

Once in the car, Macy drove steadily through Snuggler's Cove and toward Mt. Dashton. Hilda chattered about events in town, but Brianna hardly heard a word. She fidgeted in her seat until Macy glanced at her.

"We're almost there," Macy said during a rare break in Hilda's words. "Chill. We have two hours until the ferry leaves. There's time."

Brianna forced her breath out through pursed lips. Macy was right. They had time. If Susan's papers held anything of value, they could be back at the station in half an hour. If they didn't, well, she would go see Devon again anyway and try to convince him to take her seriously. She might be meddling in things that he felt were too big for her, but she didn't care. All she cared about was finding the true culprit—Connor, as far as she was concerned—and making sure he was somewhere he couldn't hurt her or anyone else ever again.

At the fork in Susan's driveway, Macy turned left toward the house instead of toward the barn. It took Hilda a solid two minutes to gather her things and exit the car. Brianna glued on a pleasant expression even as she was dancing with impatience inside. Macy shot her a few amused glances as they waited.

Hilda ambled toward the front door, its solidly expensive oak gleaming with shiny stain. "By the way, Macy, I meant to ask how Oaklyn is."

Brianna hovered behind the other two while they chatted about Macy's teenaged daughter and Hilda fumbled in her purse for her keys. Eventually, Hilda pushed the right key into Susan's door and swung it open. She shuffled into the entryway and Brianna followed on her heels.

The house was tastefully and expensively appointed. Persian rugs on the gleaming hardwood floors were clearly authentic and plush under Brianna's socked feet once she hastily took off her shoes. After renovating the Golden Moon, Brianna now knew how much Susan's light fixtures likely cost, and a glimpse of the kitchen appliances through an open entryway cemented Brianna's opinion that Susan had enjoyed the finer things in life.

"What did Susan do for a living?" she asked Hilda in a hushed voice. Brianna wasn't superstitious, but it felt strange to speak of the dead woman in her own house. She shook herself. They were here to snoop in Susan's papers. She couldn't get squeamish now.

"She didn't work," Hilda said, leading them down a hallway into an office with a view of the forest in back. "Where she got her money, no one knows. I've heard rumors of a deceased husband from before she moved to the island, or an inheritance, or even a former job as a successful runway model." Hilda tittered then covered her mouth with a sheepish look. "Excuse me, I shouldn't laugh at the dead. But you have to admit, that last rumor is highly unlikely."

Macy bit her lip, and Brianna muscled her face into an appearance of solemnity. Susan was an unlikely choice for a model, although people could change drastically. Still, it was curious that no one knew Susan's secrets. She'd hidden far more than she'd revealed. Hopefully, her documents would shed more light.

"Here are the papers I told you about," Hilda said

with a wave at a desk in the corner. It was an old-fashioned rolltop desk that Brianna would bet her café had been closed before Hilda's first visit.

Hilda's curiosity was Brianna's opportunity, though, so she didn't complain, merely sat in front of the desk and pawed through the papers.

"Here." She handed a stack to Macy. "Look through this pile for anything related to Owen, Connor, or anything suspicious. I'll go through this set."

Macy took her pile and sat in a wingback chair in the corner. Hilda sank with a sigh on the matching wingback that bookended a gas fireplace.

"Do you think Connor Pearce is embroiled in all this?" Hilda shook her head, her eyes gleaming with acquisitional glee. "A quiet man, reserved to the point of abruptness, I'd say. Brought the B&B plenty of business, what with his weekslong stay and all his meals, but getting more than two words out of him is a trial. He says he goes hiking most days, but the island is only so big. How can he find enough hikes for a week and a half? Maybe I can't imagine it because my legs wouldn't hold up for that long anymore. When I was a young woman, maybe."

Brianna nodded vaguely and tuned out Hilda's prattle. Susan, for all her tidy mind, was not organized when it came to paperwork. Receipts for groceries, letters from credit card companies, and subscription notices for magazines were jumbled together in a messy pile on the desktop.

The papers Hilda had mentioned were on top, however, and Brianna started with those. She scanned the printed email when she saw Owen Montague's email address.

You've gone too far, the note from Owen read. *You've been blackmailing me for years, and I've had enough. Everyone wants something from me, even that Connor Pearce fellow. He'll be after you once he finds out, the thieving bastard. And you can bet I'll tell him where my money's going. I'm sick of you milking me for cash, so you might as well get your share of Pearce's anger. When I sell the property, I'm leaving here, and you'll never see me again.*

Chapter 22

Brianna sat back, winded. Susan DeVries had been blackmailing Owen Montague. What secrets had she known? If both hadn't died, Brianna would have accepted this email in Susan's rolltop desk as substantial evidence for each one's guilt. If Owen was Susan's cash cow, she wouldn't have killed him, and Owen was already dead when Susan was killed. Since they clearly weren't the culprits, what did Connor Pearce want from Owen and why would he have come after Susan?

"Ah, you found it." Hilda nodded vigorously. "It was a funny sort of email, wasn't it? I don't know what the talk of blackmail was all about. That's a nasty word to throw around."

Macy darted to Brianna's side and scanned the email. Her face darkened.

"That's pretty damning evidence," she said to Brianna. "It ties Connor to both victims. Surely, that's enough for the police to interview Connor, at the very least."

Brianna stood up, the email gripped in her tight fingers. Her heart pounded with urgency. Time was ticking, and she needed to show this email to Devon. Macy was right. Surely, this was enough for the detectives to question Connor and hopefully get to the bottom of this mess.

"Let's go," Brianna said. To Hilda, she said, "Thank

you, Mrs. Button. I appreciate you letting us in here."

"Let me know what happens," she said with a bright eye. "Inquiring minds want to know!"

Macy drove at reckless speeds through the wooded section around Mt. Dashton. Hilda made little whooping noises of delight in the front seat and clutched her purse with tight fingers. Brianna didn't chastise Macy, but merely held on with grim resolve to the grab handle. If a cop pulled them over, then that was one step closer to apprehending Connor. She'd prefer to speak to Devon, but at this stage, she would take whoever she could get. It was already three thirty, and the five o'clock ferry would leave soon. If they wanted a chance at taking Connor in, she and Macy needed to give Devon their evidence pronto.

After dropping Hilda off at the Bumblebee, Macy wheeled into the parking lot of city hall and screeched to a stop in a free spot. Brianna leaped out as soon as the car halted and ran to the police station, Macy close behind.

"Is Corporal Devon Moore here?" Brianna gasped to the officer at the front counter, who stared at her with bewilderment. "I need to speak with him. Urgently."

The officer stared a moment longer, but she eventually shook her head and turned around.

"Devon," she called through the open door behind

her. "Someone here to see you."

Devon stepped out, holding his cap like he was about to leave the station. His eyes landed on Brianna, and his cheeks flushed with the barest hint of color. But when he noticed her impatient state, his brows contracted.

"Ms. West?" he said. "Come in, this way. You too, Ms. Jones."

Brianna and Macy followed Devon into the same room where she'd spoken to Devon in private before. As soon as Devon closed the door, Brianna shoved the email into his hands. She ignored the tingling of her skin when her fingers briefly brushed his. Had he contrived for their hands to meet?

"Here's your evidence." She jabbed her finger on the email with a tap that threatened to poke a hole in the flimsy paper. "But we need to act quickly."

Devon read the paper, his frown growing more pronounced with every second. His hands tightened on the paper, and Brianna's chest expanded with relief. Finally, he would believe her.

"We talked to Connor Pearce earlier today," Macy said with a glance at Brianna. "He didn't say anything that took suspicion away from him."

"And he pretended that Dot Dubois is his aunt," Brianna said hotly. "And she isn't, because she's *my* aunt, and I know everyone on that side of the family. There must be some connection, because Dot is definitely covering for him, but I don't know what it is, and Dot's not talking."

Devon rubbed his hand over his eyes. "You two went to talk to a murder suspect," he said faintly. "On your own."

"Yes," Brianna didn't want to dwell on that point, because the disapproval emitting from the Mountie was almost tangible. "And now he might leave the island. If you want to interview him, you'll need to do it before the five o'clock ferry."

Devon's eyes snapped to Brianna's face then to a clock on the wall. His lips tightened into a thin line.

"This is good evidence." He waved the paper in midair. "I'll pass it along to the detectives. But speaking to potential culprits is their job. Don't do that again, okay?"

Brianna glared at him. "You wouldn't have Connor as a suspect if it weren't for me."

"No, but—" Devon heaved a sigh and glanced at the clock again. "We'll need to set up a checkpoint at the ferry terminal, I expect. We'll bring him in and follow up with this blackmail business. It's a good lead."

Brianna looked at Macy with triumph, and Macy smiled back. They'd done it. Devon and the Mounties would finally get Connor Pearce in for questioning. Given that pointed email, they had plenty of ammunition to work with. The justice system might be slow and need a little help from time to time, but Brianna had faith that it would prevail. She let out a sigh of relief. No more watching over her shoulder for murderers, no more stabbed cheese threats in her kitchen, no more "accidents" involving bovine hooves. She could get back to her new, peaceful life on Driftwood Island.

The officer from the front counter burst into their room after a brief, frantic knock.

"Fire alarm at the community hall," she said. "Lenox and Taber are still at the north island call from earlier."

Devon cursed once she left, then he looked at the clock again.

"I'll tell the detectives our situation as soon as I deal with this alarm," he said to Brianna. "Then we'll set up the checkpoint. Thanks for your help, you two."

Devon dashed out the door, and Macy sighed deeply.

"I can't believe we got enough evidence to prod the Mounties into action." She leaned against the wall and gazed at Brianna with a satisfied smile. "A murderer will go behind bars, thanks to us, and the families of Owen Montague and Susan DeVries will have justice."

Brianna nodded, but her mind turned over the facts. Something still wasn't quite sitting right, but she couldn't put her finger on what.

"We still don't know why Susan was blackmailing Owen," she said slowly. "Or how Owen and Connor know each other."

"It will all come out in the wash," Macy said with a sage nod, "once they have Connor in custody. I'm sure he has all the answers. In the meantime, I'll pop by the Bumblebee right now and see if Connor has checked out yet. I'll let you know what I find out."

"Great idea. I'll go home, I guess. Check on the café first, maybe." Now that she didn't have a murder to solve, Brianna remembered her other primary objective, the upcoming grand opening of her café. Now that she wasn't afraid to be alone with Shaun Bartley, she could get some much-needed painting done.

Macy dropped her off in town, and Brianna walked

slowly past storefronts toward her café, her mind still whirling. A piece was missing from this puzzle, she was sure of it. That email might be strong evidence that Connor was the culprit, but it wasn't definitive proof, not yet. She wanted something more to lock him away for good. Why had he argued with Owen Montague? Why had Owen expected Connor to come after Susan?

Connor's bitter expression as he described his status as an outsider tugged at her heartstrings, but Brianna steeled herself. If he wanted sympathy, then he shouldn't be stabbing people with pitchforks and prodding water buffalos toward unsuspecting landlords.

There had to be more to discover about the developer's deal with Owen and how Connor Pearce was connected to it. Had Owen been planning to pay off Connor—or whoever Connor was working for—with the funds from selling the Montague property? Killing Owen would put an unnecessary speedbump in those plans, but Tansy could sell the property just as well. What were Connor's secret motives?

How could she find out more? Brianna's eyes glanced at the shops she passed, and her heart jumped at the next one along. A sign hung on the realtor's office door, detailing their closure on Sundays.

Brianna kept walking, but at the corner she turned and strode with quick steps to the back alley of the shop row. At the back of the realtor's shop, Brianna tried a door tucked between a trashcan and an empty parking spot. A smile grew on her face when the door creaked open. Thank goodness for trusting small towns. The door would never have been unlocked in Vancouver.

Brianna tiptoed inside, just in case someone was still around, but the shop was empty. No one sat at the two desks, one with neat piles of papers and the other clear except for a computer monitor and a framed photo of the teenaged Joel. Watercolor landscapes hung on the walls looked familiar, and Brianna recognized them as vistas from Driftwood Island: Mt. Dashton in the mist, Snuggler's Cove on a sunny summer's day, a whale breaching off Tucker Point.

The sound of footsteps out the front made Brianna freeze, her breath held. A man with a wide-brimmed straw hat sauntered by the glass window and disappeared. Brianna melted against the wall then stood straight with an inhale. She didn't know how long she had before someone noticed her snooping in the closed office, so she walked straight to a filing cabinet and flipped through tabs on file folders with twitching fingers.

There was nothing under M for Montague, but the name "Raven Ridge Golf" caught her eye. She pulled out the file and scanned the contents. Inside were artist renditions of a golf course on a landscape she vaguely recognized as the Montague's property. A large pond sketched near the road curdled Brianna's stomach with anger, and she flipped to the next sheet of paper.

This was a title for the sale of a property, and Owen Montague's name was on the top. Nothing had been signed yet. A large sticky note in neat handwriting said, "Sale paused on request of Tansy Montague following death of Owen Montague."

Brianna shivered with a chill that had nothing to do

with the warm summer's late afternoon. Tansy didn't want the sale of her land to go through, and Owen clearly had. Suspicions that Brianna hadn't truly entertained until now slotted into place. Tansy Montague's bloody apron the morning of Owen's murder. Her protectiveness of her son Jay, who clearly loved the farm and their water buffalo business. The family's tension-filled connection with Susan DeVries, who now lay in the morgue.

The receipt for the Bumblebee. Brianna's mind flicked to the first time she'd met Tansy Montague, the morning she'd had to break the news of Owen's death. Tansy had been holding a pastel-striped takeaway cup filled with a smoothie from Hilda's B&B, the same order as the receipt trampled into Susan's murder site.

Hilda had said that many of the islanders were creatures of habit. Tansy's morning smoothie must have been one of them. Brianna was willing to bet that Tansy had visited the Bumblebee the morning of Owen's death.

"Tansy Montague is the murderer," Brianna said out loud into the silence of the realty office. Once she said it, it felt right. As Dot had said, it was often the ones closest to the victims that had enough motive for murder. As Owen's wife, Tansy was one of the closest. Her heart pounded with her revelation.

Something sharp pressed into Brianna's back, and she froze.

"Should have kept your prying to yourself," Tansy's sharp voice said from behind her.

Chapter 23

Brianna tried to turn, but the knife that was poking into the soft part of her lower back forced itself deeper until her shirt tore, and the pressure turned into sharp pain. Brianna hissed and stayed still.

"Yeah," Tansy said with smug satisfaction in her voice. "I'm a farm girl, born and raised. Trust me, I know how to use a knife, and blood doesn't bother me one bit."

"What are you doing, Tansy?" Brianna whispered, but her sinking heart told her what her mind didn't want to comprehend.

"Silencing you," she said. "You're the nosiest little baker I've ever had the misfortune of meeting, and that's saying something on this gossipy island. Your meddling aunt decided to confess to Owen's murder. If you hadn't been around to stick your nose into places it shouldn't be, the whole thing would have been too perfect for words. But, no, you had to butt in, didn't you?"

"To defend my innocent aunt against your crimes?" Brianna choked out. Her blood pounded in her ears until she could barely hear herself think. "Yeah, and I don't regret it."

"They'll pin it on Connor Pearce," Tansy said with confidence. "Your accusations are perfect for that. And I left a little evidence of my own at the police station—anonymously, of course—and that insider information of Connor's involvement will be the linchpin in that bastard's case."

"Don't talk about him like that," Brianna snapped. Now that she knew Connor wasn't the murderer, the sympathy she'd tried to bottle up earlier welled inside her. "There's no need to call him names."

Tansy grabbed her arm and marched her toward the door.

"No funny movements," she warned. "And no calling out for help. I know exactly where to cut you so you'll bleed out before the ambulance gets here. It's a skill that comes with slaughtering animals on our farm. I might go to jail, but Jay will be safe and taken care of." She pressed the knife harder into Brianna. "Got it?"

Brianna nodded, even as her eyes raked the area for something, anything, that could help her defend against Tansy's knife. She didn't think she was quick enough to avoid a stab, though, so she stumbled beside Tansy and out the door toward a low-slung, flashy red sports car. Brianna glanced at the tires with their asymmetrical tread pattern, and her stomach cramped with recognition. They matched the tire tracks in Susan's dirt perfectly.

Tansy saw Brianna looking at the expensive car. "It's my friend Grace's," she explained. "She's been unwittingly helping me all along. She's such a pushover that she didn't even ask why I wanted to borrow her car. And that night when Susan died in her field? I visited Grace right before—to borrow her car—and changed her clocks so that she would be my alibi if the police came knocking. Clever, right?"

Brianna didn't dignify Tansy's boast with a response.

Instead, she glanced around the alley, but no one was around to cry out to for help. After Tansy shoved Brianna into the backseat, she strapped Brianna's wrists together with zip ties. Brianna tried to struggle, but Tansy's long carving knife sliced her on the forearm with agonizing pain, and she desisted.

She berated herself for getting into this situation. Devon was right. Greg's voice in her head spoke the truth. She didn't belong here, sticking her nose in where she could do no good. She should have stayed in her café. Or, better yet, stayed in her consulting job in Vancouver, where she knew what to do and when to do it. She'd only made a mess of things here—driving Connor Pearce off the island, allowing Tansy to threaten and now kidnap her—and she regretted not heeding Greg's lessons. She really was useless in this situation without training. She should have left the investigation to the professionals.

Once Tansy was in the front seat and driving, she continued as if they had been speaking the whole time.

"I called Connor Pearce a bastard, but it's not name-calling if it's true," she said in her shrill voice. "Connor is Owen's bastard child from before we met. I didn't find out until the other day. That information was too good not to pass along to the police. The cast-off son, back for revenge? It was perfect. Connor had the audacity to claim parentage—and the inheritance to go with it—from Owen. Like I'd let him ever see a dime that should be Jay's."

Brianna blinked at the back of Tansy's head. Was that why Susan had seen Connor and Owen yelling at each other? If Owen hadn't ever acknowledged Connor, and

Connor had finally confronted his father, Brianna could imagine tensions being high. Her shoulders slumped at the thought of the pain Connor must have been going through, and she wished she could take back the accusations she'd flung in his face. If she got out of this alive, she wouldn't stop until Connor was out of danger of arrest.

"You killed your husband," Brianna said, wanting to get her facts straight. She'd been wrapped up in this mystery for too long to not want the answers, even if she were in danger of never telling anyone else about them. She swallowed hard. "And made Jay cover for you as an alibi, I presume."

"Don't bring my darling boy into this," Tansy said. "He has no idea what I did. Not that he mourned Owen much—the man never had anything good to say of his own son—but Jay is innocent."

"Why did you kill Owen? Because he had a child you never knew about? His affair with Diana drove you to revenge? Because he wanted to sell your farm?"

"It shouldn't have been his to sell," she hissed, her knuckles white on the steering wheel. Mt. Dashton loomed in front of them. "I should have got half if he ever tried to leave me. But his connections in the stock trading world—well, let's just say that insider trading gained him loyal friends with legal backgrounds. I had no idea—I was too young and stupid when we married—but he tied up his assets in an air-tight pre-nuptial agreement, including this Driftwood property that he inherited from his father—so I'd be left with nothing." Tansy glanced in the rearview mirror, her eyes narrowed with hate. "He came home one day and announced he was going to leave me for Diana Bartley. He and that floozy were going to sell the farm and leave Driftwood Island with the money. We didn't need him around—he was a terrible father and husband, no loss there—but Jay and I would have had hardly any money left. And the water buffalo business? It might have been Owen's cover story, but it's Jay's livelihood, and his pride and joy. His own father was going to rip that away from him. Can you imagine?"

Tansy was practically spitting at this point. The car swerved into the other lane before Tansy got control of the vehicle again, and Brianna's head banged against the window with the jerky motions.

"But why Susan?" Brianna said, still wanting to get answers despite her new pounding headache. "What was the blackmail about?"

Tansy huffed a short, sharp laugh. "Yet another thing that my dear husband never deigned to share with me. I tell you, men who want you to stay in the kitchen, they're the worst. If he'd told me more, I could have dug us out of this hole he'd dropped us in. But no, I wasn't *clever* enough to understand anything." Her voice dripped with sarcasm, and Brianna winced. Tansy hadn't solved her issues in an ethical way, but Brianna could empathize with where she'd come from a little too well.

"Susan DeVries," Tansy continued, "had somehow wormed out of Owen where he'd made his money before coming to the island. I knew about the illegal trading—I'd been dating him at the time—but we'd been so careful when we moved here to keep it a secret. The law would have caught up with us eventually if we hadn't taken precautions. Owen changed his surname to mine, we retrained everyone who knew him as a teenager on Driftwood Island, and we started the water buffalo business to cement ourselves in the community. Can you imagine the hammer that would have fallen on us if the searching authorities had found out where we were?"

Tansy changed gears, and the sports car roared faster. Brianna swallowed and glanced out the window and the forbidding trees at the foot of Mt. Dashton. Part of her was soaking up every syllable of Tansy's explanation—it was so good to hear what was going on behind the scenes—but the other, larger part of her was terrified for where this afternoon would end. She'd reached her limits, she knew, and Greg's voice in her head was louder than it had ever been. She shouldn't have meddled. She might be finding out the truth, but at what cost?

"Susan had Owen by the throat, and she knew it," Tansy continued, clearly relishing the chance to detail her crafty plans to someone. "She was clever, I'll give her that. With the blackmail, she set herself up for a lifetime of extra funds. That's why we rented her pond for the water buffalo, apparently. There were other, better options, but Owen insisted. I went through his papers last week, after he died, and I found the payments for leasing the land. Way more than we should have been paying. It was clearly a front for laundering the blackmail money."

"So, what? You wanted to make a clean sweep of it with Susan?" Brianna asked. Her eyes raked the backseat of the car for something, anything, to cut her zip ties.

"If Susan had been smarter, she would have dropped it with Owen's death." Tansy shook her head, and her blond bob wiggled with the motion. "But she came to my house with a demand to continue the blackmail relationship. I chased her off the property, but she threatened to expose us. I couldn't have that—for Jay's sake—so I borrowed Grace's car to cover my tracks, just in case, and drove to Susan's house. I chased her into the water buffalo pen, trying to talk sense into her, but she wasn't having it. Susan threatened to call the cops. All her shouting spooked the water buffalo, and that's when I got the idea of how to silence Susan. There's a cattle prod in the barn, so I grabbed that and forced the buffalo to run her over. She wasn't quite dead yet, so I stuck the prod into her chest until her heart stopped."

Tansy was panting after her explanation like she'd run a race. Brianna could only stare at the back of her blond head in horror. She'd known that Tansy had murdered Susan, but what a cold, terrible way to go.

"And what are you planning to do with me?" Brianna said, trying and failing to keep her voice steady.

"The stampede worked great with Susan." Tansy pulled into Susan's driveway and bumped along the dirt track. "No reason I can't do the same thing again. I'll plant some clues to frame someone else, though, in case the police think it's not an accident. Maybe Hilda's daughter. She can't be liking the thought of your new café taking away some of her business. Yes, that will do nicely."

Tansy's large handbag was on the console between the front seats. Brianna stared at it for a moment. It was her only chance at finding something to break free of the zip ties. She couldn't let Tansy kill her. She couldn't let her win and walk away without justice being served.

When Tansy glanced toward Susan's farmhouse, Brianna acted. She reached forward and slid the purse onto her lap. Feverishly, her bound hands pawed through the contents. Tissues, wallet, lipstick, none of those would do much against a zip tie.

Finally, her questing fingers found metal. She gripped the nail file in her hand and pushed the purse onto the floor of the backseat, away from her feet. Hopefully, Tansy would think the purse had slipped there by itself. Brianna sawed at the plastic trapping her wrists.

Tansy stopped the car then walked around to Brianna's side and flung the door open. Time was running out, and the zip ties were proving to be tougher than Brianna had hoped. She opened her mouth and screamed.

"Help! Anyone. Fire, Murder. Call the police!"

"Shut it," Tansy snarled. She leaned over and grabbed her purse. With trembling fingers, she rummaged through the mess until she pulled out a beige silk scarf with triumph. She shoved it in Brianna's yelling mouth until Brianna choked and grew quiet. The fabric tickled her throat and felt dry and strange on her tongue.

"Get out," Tansy commanded. "And don't even think about escape. You're done for, get it through your head. Susan's neighbors are away for the month, the road is hidden by trees, and no one else is near enough to see."

When Brianna refused to move, glaring at Tansy through her watering eyes, Tansy huffed and spun around to march to the barn. Brianna didn't have time to wonder what she was doing before she returned, clutching a long rod in her hand.

"Jay doesn't much like the cattle prod," she said. "He's a sweet boy, very fond of the animals. But sometimes you need the right tool to get the job done. Now, move."

When Brianna only stared in horror at the device in Tansy's hand, the older woman shoved it against Brianna's bare thigh below her shorts.

Fiery pain lanced through Brianna, and every muscle seized in a full-body Charlie horse. She released a tortured scream that was muffled by the scarf in her mouth.

The cramping stopped, but all her muscles had turned to jelly and twitched on their own. Tansy stepped back and waved at her impatiently. "Come on, there's plenty more where that came from. I want to get this over and done with before someone misses you. I have footprints to sweep away and evidence to plant."

She approached with the cattle prod raised again, but Brianna shuffled quickly out of her seat and stood on wobbling legs. Tansy gave a satisfied nod and pushed Brianna toward the gate with a rough hand.

Brianna tried to take deep, calming breaths through her nose, but it was a fruitless endeavor. She was well and truly stuck. No one knew where she was. No one suspected Tansy was the killer behind Owen and Susan's deaths. No one would stop her in time.

Brianna resumed her frantic sawing at the zip ties. They were very thick, and she'd only made a small dent so far in the plastic. Still, it was her only chance, so whenever Tansy looked away, Brianna continued her feverish motions.

Tansy pushed her through the water buffalo gate and across the pastureland. Long grasses tickled Brianna's bare legs, and the ground grew muddier as they walked closer to the water buffalo. A few of the animals looked up placidly, and Brianna wondered how Tansy would get them to stampede. They didn't look like they could muster up the interest to walk to the other side of the pond.

"It doesn't matter," Tansy said, seemingly reading her thoughts. "They don't need to stampede, they just need to look like they did. The stampede that did Susan in was a stroke of luck. Normally the buffalo can't be bothered to run. I'll kill you here, then I'll herd them over your body to make it look like they did the job. By the time they're done, no one will see the cattle prod mark on your chest."

Brianna closed her eyes briefly. She wondered if they had done the autopsy on the other woman yet.

She glared at Tansy, still unable to speak through the gag. Her hands worked overtime on the zip tie. She was so close, now...

"What are you doing?" Tansy cried. She batted at Brianna's hands, and the nail file slipped through her fingers. Brianna watched with horror as the file glinted in the evening sun on its way to the ground. Now she had no chance of escape. Her only hope was that Devon and Macy would think her death suspicious. Hopefully, the matching autopsy reports from her and Susan's bodies would trigger a closer look. The thought didn't give her much consolation.

Tansy raised the cattle prod, her mouth set with determination. "It didn't have to be this way," she said. "You could have kept your nose out of my business. But I have to do this, for Jay's sake. This is for his future. Goodbye, Brianna."

Chapter 24

Brianna stared at Tansy, her mind blank and her limbs trembling. Tansy held the cattle prod closer to Brianna's chest, and she braced for impact. Her last thought was one of regret for the waste of her new life here. She'd thought she'd turned everything around, but it had all been for nothing.

"Stop!" A man yelled, his voice filled with panic.

Tansy glanced toward the barn. Brianna didn't hesitate, didn't even turn to look at the newcomer. Her bound hands shot forward and knocked the cattle prod away from her chest. She slammed her wrists against her bent knee, and the weakened zip tie snapped.

Tansy turned with a snarl, but Brianna snatched the cattle prod from her hands and turned it around so the live end faced Tansy. The other woman's face changed from menacing to fearful in an instant. Brianna pulled the scarf from her mouth and dropped it in the mud at her feet.

"Put your hands up, Tansy Montague," Brianna said in a steady voice. Righteous indignation flowed through her, along with a healthy helping of adrenaline. The killer was in her control, and Brianna wasn't going to die today. "You're going to the police, right now."

"We're already here," Devon's voice said sternly as he approached from the barn. Brianna didn't take her eyes off Tansy—she'd heard enough stories from Greg about what happened when crooks thought the police weren't looking—but she couldn't help the relieved smile that overtook her face. She watched in satisfaction as Devon clipped a set of handcuffs around Tansy's unresisting wrists. Only then did she drop the cattle prod and rub her face with shaking hands.

"Take Tansy to the car, will you?" Devon said to Lenox.

Lenox led the murderer away, and two detectives—a tall woman with short hair and the paunchy man Brianna had spotted earlier—approached Tansy as they walked. Devon turned to Brianna with concern radiating from his face. He touched her shoulder, and the warmth from his hand spreading through her thin shirt like a sunbeam at the beach. He left his hand there for longer than Brianna expected him to, but she felt no desire to complain.

Devon peered into her face, his warm eyes searching hers intently. "Are you all right?"

"I will be," Brianna told him honestly. "That was a close one."

"This is why I warned you away from the investigation," he growled. His hand gripped her shoulder tighter. "That was way too close."

"But I solved the case!" Brianna stepped away from Devon and put her hands on her hips. How could he berate her after that? "Tansy would still be running around, murdering whomever she liked. Actually, if I hadn't snooped around, my innocent aunt would likely still be in custody. I know you don't think I'm capable enough to mess with your business, but I think I deserve a modicum of credit for that."

"Not capable?" Devon stared at Brianna, then he ran his hands through his hair until the usually tamed strands stood on end. It made him look younger and vulnerable in a way that Brianna liked to see. "I think you're far too capable, that's the problem. You were finding clues left, right, and center, and you struck to the heart of the investigation well before the detectives. I didn't want you there because I didn't want you to become a target. I wanted to keep you safe."

Brianna bit her lip. Well, that was certainly not what she had expected. She'd prematurely painted Devon with the same brush as Greg. Her bruised ego glowed with his praise.

"You agree that I helped?" she said quietly.

Devon's eyes softened. "Immeasurably. In fact, Hilda Button called the detachment after remembering whose receipt it was that you found in the field. When Tansy Montague wasn't at her home, I offered to check the water buffalo field, thanks to your suspicions that Susan's death was murder. The detectives figure that Tansy doused Owen with an extra sleeping pill to make him woozy that morning, and when she snuck up behind him with the pitchfork, he didn't react fast enough to stop her."

"He had earbuds in," Brianna recalled. "He probably didn't even hear her. It would have been relatively simple to get the drop on Owen in that state."

"Exactly."

"But why frame Dot?" Brianna stared at Devon while her mind clicked over. "It must have been a happy opportunity of the moment. Tansy wanted to hurt Owen, then she saw Dot's pitchfork leaning against the fence and figured it would take the heat off her."

"And with a pair of work gloves—easy enough to come by on a farm—she wouldn't even have left prints on the tool." Devon raised an eyebrow at Brianna. "Now, can I please drive you home where you won't antagonize any more murderers, at least for today?"

Brianna laughed, long and hard, letting the insanity of the past hour wash away in the sound. Devon smiled with concern still in his eyes.

"Yes," she said finally. "Yes, I'm ready to go."

Devon drove Brianna to Dot's house, and she texted Macy on the way. Dot ran out of the house with open arms when Brianna stepped out of the police cruiser, and Macy followed close behind. Brianna didn't realize Devon was leaving until gravel crunched under his tires.

There would be time to thank him for the ride home later, she reasoned, caught in her aunt's and friend's embraces. Thanks to his timely intervention and her quick reflexes, Brianna had many more days on Driftwood Island to look forward to. She squeezed Dot and Macy tighter, finally allowing herself to relax into their warmth and let the tension and adrenaline of the past hour—the past week—drain out of her body.

"Tea," Dot said finally, wiping a tear from her eye.

"That's what we need. Too bad we don't have any of your baking."

"Yes, she was a little preoccupied today," Macy said. They all chuckled, then Macy looked sheepish. "Although, I might have grabbed the cheese buns you left on the café counter, Brianna. I thought we might need them to butter people up during questioning."

"Then a proper teatime it is," Dot cried. "Come inside, you two. It's getting chilly now the sun is almost down."

Brianna glanced at the setting sun, which spilled luscious pinks and vibrant oranges across puffy clouds and into the inky blue of the coming night. The sun was setting, but the gorgeous end of today promised a hopeful new day to come. Brianna would be there to greet it, ready to step forward into her new life with confidence. She didn't need to listen to the voice in her head that told her she wasn't smart enough or capable enough to handle things. It had been a tight squeeze to escape the clutches of Tansy Montague today, but she'd done it, and solved the murders to boot.

Brianna took a deep breath and released everything in a long sigh. Then, she followed Dot and Macy into the house, ready to put her feet up with tea and a cheese bun.

The kettle was on, and Macy bustled in the kitchen, finding plates for the buns. Brianna took off her shoes and glanced at her aunt, who was searching for teacups.

"Dot," she said. "Are you going to tell us why you confessed to the murder of Owen Montague?"

Dot froze with her hand on a cupboard door. She slowly turned toward Brianna with her brow furrowed, twisting her hands together.

"Brianna," she said with hesitation. "There's something I want to tell you. In fact, maybe it would be better to show you." She raised her voice. "Connor, could you please come out, darling?"

Brianna blinked as Connor Pearce emerged from the hallway where she knew Dot's spare bedroom was. He glanced at Brianna with suspicion then looked at Dot, who waved him closer to her.

"This is my son." Dot slid her arm through Connor's and gripped it as if she couldn't bear to let him go. "I was with him the morning of Owen's murder. I was afraid he would be accused of the crime, so I confessed to protect him."

Brianna stopped breathing. Her eyes darted between the two faces, and she didn't know how she hadn't realized it before. Connor had Dot's pale hair and long nose, and shared Brianna's own hazel irises. His eyes held suspicion and skepticism instead of Dot's open curiosity, but otherwise, they were clearly related.

"I don't know what to ask first," Brianna said at last. "Where has he been? How did I not know about him?"

Dot's eyes filled with tears, and she clutched Connor closer. He looked down at their connection but didn't pull away.

"I dated Owen Montague in high school," she said in a wavering voice. "When I got pregnant, he wanted nothing to do with me or the baby. It wasn't easy to abort in those days, and I was so young to keep the baby, so my parents sent me to a family friend of theirs who lived in Sechelt."

Brianna glanced at Connor—that was why his hometown in the Bumblebee's guestbook stated Sechelt—but he kept his eyes on his mother.

"A nice family adopted him, I was told," Dot continued, her voice growing stronger. "I thought he would have a good life, better than I could have given him. It was a closed adoption—most were in those days—so I never knew what had happened to him." She clutched her chest with her free hand like she could hold the pieces of her breaking heart together.

Connor picked up the story when it was clear Dot couldn't continue. "They died in a ski lift accident when I was five. I was shuffled into foster care, where I bounced around until I was sixteen. Not exactly the warm, nurturing environment Dot was hoping for, I imagine."

Dot buried her face in her son's shoulder and spoke in a muffled voice. "When they started to allow postings to connect adopted children with their birth parents, I signed up right away. This was years ago, now, but Connor looked me up a few months ago."

"A friend of mine had a baby," Connor said with a shrug. "It got me thinking about all that. Thought it couldn't hurt to explore." He scowled. "Meeting Owen was not a highlight, to say the least. What a jerk. Threatened to run me off the property with his truck if I didn't stop bothering him. Afraid of his wife, I think."

"Apparently, he was right to be afraid," Macy said quietly. She placed plates on a tray and filled the teapot with hot water. "Although she didn't kill him entirely for that reason."

Brianna stepped forward gingerly. She eyed Connor with interest. A swell of emotion that she couldn't name blossomed in her chest.

"You're my cousin," she said, testing the word out. At Connor's nervous look, she smiled widely. "That's amazing. New family. Welcome, Connor. It's so nice to know you. I'm sorry we got off on the wrong foot."

"Yeah, well, I'm used to it." Connor shuffled, and Dot squeezed his arm tighter. He looked pleased at Brianna's words, though, and Brianna couldn't stop grinning.

"Tea's ready," Macy said. "And the cheese buns are warm. Let's dig in, new family."

Something thudded against the porch glass door. Brianna jumped and peered into the dusky night. A white figure stared in with unblinking yellow eyes.

"Zola?" Dot chuckled and walked to the door. "You crazy critter. Wanted to join the party, no doubt. Hay is better for you, my love."

"Connor." Brianna waved him forward and he stepped toward her with hesitation. "Since you're part of the family now, you'd better learn what the incredible escaping Zola eats. Want to help me put her in the barn?"

His eyes softened when he looked at the animal.

"Sure," he said quietly. "I'll meet Dot's other kid."

Chapter 25

Magnus Pickleton rapped his knuckles on a folding table in the community hall three days later.

"Order, order," he called out in a voice loud enough to halt a roomful of chattering crowds.

Instead, Quentin and Esmerelda finished their quiet conversation, and Hilda closed her lips with a prim smile after regaling Brianna with a blow-by-blow account of her latest guests' antics. The room grew silent, and Magnus graced them with a sanctimonious nod, a fleck of what looked like a cracker lodged firmly in his beard.

"Welcome to the first June meeting of the Gourmand Society. We have suffered losses and disruptions to our usual proceedings of late." He glanced at the spot where Susan had used to sit. "But we must carry on with our appreciation and advocacy of the artisan food industry of Driftwood Island, the way Susan would want us to. First order of business. Is there any news from members?"

Hilda pointed her darning needle at Brianna, a large green sock dangling from her other hand. "Go on, dear. Tell us what happened during the kerfuffle with Tansy Montague."

"That's not food-related," Magnus protested.

"I disagree," Esmerelda said loftily. "Tansy Montague is an integral part of the water buffalo business, which provides milk for our local mozzarella. News of her incarceration is of vital importance to the Gourmand Society."

"And I need more details," Hilda said with a stern look at Magnus. "Especially since I was the one who helped find clues and point young Corporal Moore in the right direction."

When Magnus subsided with a huff, Esme winked at Brianna, who took that as her cue to summarize the events of the last two weeks. The Gourmand Society members were suitably enthralled, and Brianna tried to weave her tale into one worthy of being told. She didn't mention the revelation of Connor's parentage—that was up to Dot and Connor to divulge—but she told them the rest, including her standoff in the water buffalo field.

"What will happen to the water buffalo?" she asked once her tale was complete. "Now that Owen is dead and Tansy is under trial for murder?"

"I spoke to young Jay yesterday at the car stop." Hilda leaned forward with her news. "He's determined to rise above his family's tragedies and keep the business going. I don't doubt a lot of his spunk is from denial of his new situation, so he'll bear watching for when it all sinks in. He's very young, but that comes with a healthy dose of determination. Apparently, he's the one who does most of the day-to-day work with the buffalo. He might need a guiding hand with the business side of things, but if you ask me, he might pull it off."

"Good," Magnus said with the same satisfaction he might show if he'd personally overseen Jay's work. "Then our mozzarella is not under immediate threat."

"And a good thing, too," Brianna added. "Since I'm

making it a centerpiece of my grand opening. I thought Jay could use all the help he could get, so I ordered a big batch from their cheesemaker."

"When's the big day?" Esme asked.

"So glad you asked," Brianna said. She pulled out flyers from her purse with a flourish and passed them around. They depicted a cheese board and colorful lettering detailing the Golden Moon's grand opening. "It's this Saturday, and you're all invited. All profits from the grand opening will go toward buying art supplies for Happy Hearts preschool."

"I suppose I could pop by," Magnus said gruffly.

Hilda shook her head at him and turned to Brianna. "We'll be there," she said with a smile. "All of us."

The Golden Moon was jammed, with every table filled and more customers entering all the time. Oaklyn filled coffee orders in a café-branded tee shirt, her brow furrowed with concentration on her task instead of surliness. Macy's daughter had turned up in torn black fishnets and a low-cut cropped shirt, but Brianna had prepared for that. Now, they both wore matching yellow shirts with a picture of a Swiss cheese wedge on the front. Macy was there as well, flitting between tables and greeting everyone she knew.

Brianna ran between the kitchen and counter to keep the baking trays filled for Oaklyn. Any time she had a breather, she circulated the dining room and introduced herself. It felt odd to Brianna—her big-city years had conditioned her to keep strangers at arm's length—but most people she spoke to greeted her with friendliness.

"This scone is just delicious," an elderly woman with purple-rinsed hair gushed to her when she offered a coffee refill on the house. "Divine."

Brianna accepted the compliment graciously and moved to the next table, barely able to keep a grin from splitting her face in two. The busyness made her feel vibrant and alive in a way she'd rarely encountered in her previous life. Had everyone turned up for the grand opening? She didn't want to presume that this number of customers would continue past today, but it was the best start she could possibly give her little cheese café. After this, the quality of her products would have to do the work for her.

The open door darkened as new customers arrived. Brianna had a moment between jobs, so she walked forward to greet the newcomers. She smiled when she recognized the Gourmand Society.

"Hello, dear," Hilda said fondly from her position in the vanguard. "We're here in full force. Look, even Magnus came."

Brianna nodded at the grumpy president, who muttered a greeting. Esme and Quentin said hello, and Brianna looked around.

"It's pretty busy today—oh, look, there's a table free just now. Let me clean it off and you can sit there."

Brianna whisked behind the counter, grabbed her spray bottle and cloth, and wiped down the glass top of the round table that covered her sunny yellow tablecloths. While the others settled in their seats, Magnus followed her to the counter, where Oaklyn leaned against the wall during her first pause of the day. She looked wide-eyed at the full restaurant, and Brianna took pity on her.

"Why don't you take your break now?" she said to the teen. "Be back here in fifteen minutes, okay?"

Oaklyn didn't need a second invitation. She fled the counter area, and Brianna heard the kitchen door slam shut behind the girl.

Brianna smiled at Magnus and spread her hands over the counter. "What can I get for you? We have asiago apricot scones, raspberry mascarpone croissants, carrot cake with cream cheese icing, and—" A timer dinged from the kitchen, and Brianna held up her finger. "And fresh rosemary and paprika mozzarella bites made with Montague buffalo milk."

Magnus sniffed and glanced at the offerings behind glass.

"I'd better order the mozzarella," he said gruffly. "What with recent events and all. Hilda will have my hide if I don't support young Jay."

Brianna took Magnus's credit card and rang his purchase through with a suppressed smile.

"I'll bring the bites right out to your table," she promised. "I think you'll like them."

Magnus harumphed and stumped back to the Society. Brianna flitted into the kitchen and pushed her hands into oven mitts, then pulled a tray of breaded cheese bites out of her oven, which was working without a hitch as if it knew how important today was. The breading was a perfect golden brown, flecked with pieces of green rosemary leaves. Brianna took a deep breath and let the aroma of melted cheese fill her nostrils. Then, she pulled out one of the empty cast iron frying pans kept warm in the oven, transferred some of the bites into it, and set the pan on a fitted heat pad.

She deposited the frying pan on the Gourmand Society's table a minute later, along with a bundle of forks wrapped in napkins. The group took a collective sniff.

"Don't mind if I do," Esme said, reaching for a fork to spear one of the mozzarella bites. "Let's see what our newest society member can accomplish with cheese."

Brianna hovered while the members prodded forks into the mozzarella and tucked pieces into their mouths. After a moment of chewing, during which Brianna tried not to fidget with her hands, Hilda swallowed.

"Just scrumptious," she said clearly. "In fact, I'll have another."

"The texture of the buffalo really stands out here," Quentin said. "It's moister than cow's, but it works with this method of cooking."

"I'm following Hilda's lead," said Esme with a grin at Brianna. She speared another bite onto her fork.

Magnus didn't meet Brianna's eye until Hilda kicked him under the table. He looked up at the cheese café owner.

"It is—" he paused to find his words. "Absolutely delicious."

Brianna grinned at him, heartened that she'd won

over the old foodie with her baking. "Glad you think so. Please, enjoy the rest."

She ducked away from the society and nearly bumped into Macy, who had just said goodbye to a couple at another table who had a toddler demolishing a scone with single-minded intensity.

"This is amazing," Macy said to her, eyes bright with excitement. "The grand opening is clearly a smashing success. Everyone I talk to can't stop raving about your food, the décor, everything. You're going places, girl."

"And plenty of profit for art supplies," Brianna replied. "Will the little food artist over there enjoy smearing paint as much as he does smearing butter?"

Macy chuckled with a glance at the toddler. "Undoubtedly. Hey, did you see Shaun and Diana Bartley are here?" She nodded at a corner table, where Shaun and a pretty woman with honey-colored wavy hair sat with a little boy tucking into a croissant. The two adults looked uncomfortable together, but when Diana laid her hand tentatively on Shaun's arm, he didn't move it away. Instead, he glanced at his wife and gave her the start of a smile.

"I think there might be hope for them," Brianna whispered to Macy. "Even after her infidelity."

"Maybe Shaun took it as a wakeup call instead of a betrayal," Macy suggested. "Diana seems penitent, anyway. Here's hoping they can work it out."

"Hey, I've been meaning to ask. Have you tasted any of Orca Vineyard's wine?" Brianna asked. "Someone at the float home party was raving about it."

"Yes, it's good. That's the stuff I had at the pub the

other night." Macy wrinkled her nose. "Surprising how Sebastian Merle's sourness doesn't affect the grapes. Maybe all the sweetness in his life gets sucked into his wine, leaving none for himself."

Brianna was about to answer, but movement at the door caught her eye. The lull was over. Since Oaklyn was on break, she needed to get back to the till.

She did a double take. Jay Montague stood by himself at the threshold, shifting from foot to foot as if unsure of his welcome. A few customers glanced at him with curiosity and a hint of hostility.

Brianna frowned then strode forward with a smile. Jay wasn't his parents, and he deserved to be treated on his own merit. From what she had seen of the young man, he was guilty of nothing more than strong adoration of his water buffalo.

"Jay," she greeted him. "Welcome to the Golden Moon."

"Hi, Ms. West." His face opened with relief at Brianna's welcome. "It looks busy in here."

"Call me Brianna, please. Come in, come in." She ushered him toward the counter. "I just pulled some mozzarella bites out of the oven. Cheese from your buffalo milk, of course. Try some on the house, see what you think."

Before Jay could protest, Brianna whisked into the kitchen and came back bearing a small frying pan with hot bites inside. Jay reached out with the impulse of a hungry young man, but his hand hesitated before grabbing a bite.

"I wanted to apologize," he said, withdrawing his arm.

Brianna put the pan and heat pad on the counter, and Jay scratched his head for something to do with his hands. "My mother almost…" his voice petered off, then he stood straighter. "Well, I'm really sorry for what happened that night. If I'd known—"

"Thank you for the apology, but it's not your fault." Brianna laid a hand on his shoulders, which slumped underneath her touch. She squeezed then removed her fingers.

"But it sort of is." He twisted his hands together, and his breath came quickly. Panic danced behind his eyes. "I covered up for my mother about my father's death."

"Are you sure you want to confess that to me?" Brianna said carefully. "You don't want to be an accessory to murder. And I'm sure your mother doesn't want you to take the fall for something she asked you to do."

"Well, she didn't ask me anything. She just took a long time feeding the egg chickens that morning while we were butchering, and the timing was right for—" He swallowed. "Well, you know. But I didn't say anything."

Brianna nodded slowly, making her mind up. "I hope you understand now to be truthful to the police if there's a murder investigation, because our actions have consequences. But you know what, I'm all about clean slates and fresh starts. Are you game?"

She stuck out her hand, and Jay shook it, gingerly at first, but with increasing firmness as his panic faded.

"A fresh start sounds good. Especially since I'm running the business now." He looked a little green. "I'll need all the friends I can get."

"If you run into trouble, I used to be a consultant for small businesses, back in Vancouver." She passed Jay the hot frying pan and he took it with a hungry look. "Just ask."

Jay moved off to find a table, and Brianna leaned against the counter for a brief respite from the madness of her grand opening. Her eyes traveled around the happy, chattering crowd, and her heart felt as full as the dining room. This was what she'd longed for: a fresh start in a new town among burgeoning friends. Her time in Snuggler's Cove had started out with a rough patch, but the future looked bright.

Dot sipped her tea at a side table across from a relaxed-looking Connor. Brianna smiled to see them together, then her breath caught as Jay approached their table. The younger man looked unsure but determined, and he stuck his hand out to Connor after some words. Was he introducing himself as Connor's half-brother?

Connor stared at Jay for a long moment, long enough that Jay's arm wavered. Then he stood and grasped Jay's hand in a tight grip while his other hand patted Jay's shoulder. Dot was beaming when she pulled a chair out for the young buffalo farmer to sit with them. Jay surreptitiously wiped his eyes on his sleeve.

Brianna sighed happily then jumped when a familiar voice spoke behind her.

"Are there any scones left?"

Brianna whirled around to face Devon Moore. He grinned at her, his face boyish with the expression and his hair falling in untamed waves above well-fitting jeans and a tight black tee shirt. Brianna's heart pattered, and she told herself that it was from Devon sneaking up on her. It definitely wasn't because of that smile.

Her heart twisted. Had she given up on Greg's memory so quickly? Then she straightened. She and Greg had been unraveling long before his death. To everything there was a season, and the Golden Moon wouldn't be her fresh start if she didn't let her past go.

Still, there was no need for her heart to thump quite so hard.

"Absolutely," she said brightly and whirled behind the counter to cover her embarrassment. "I baked an unseemly number of scones this morning."

She put one on a plate with a pat of butter in a small metal dish and passed it to Devon. He took the plate with a hungry gleam in his eye and handed her some cash.

"I'm glad you're here," he said. When she glanced quickly at him, wondering what he meant, his cheeks flushed with the faintest hint of rose. "I mean, I'm glad you opened the café. What a great addition to Snuggler's Cove."

"I'm glad I'm here, too." And Brianna meant it, every word. Now that the murders of Owen and Susan were solved, and Dot was a free woman, she had a peaceful future on this idyllic island to look forward to. Surely, two murders were enough for this small place. She smiled at Devon, who grinned back. "And I'm here to stay."

Author's Note

Driftwood Island is a fictional island based on the very real Gulf Islands, which reside between mainland British Columbia and the vastly larger Vancouver Island. I took the liberty of changing Vancouver Island's name to Victoria Island to avoid confusion, since the city of Vancouver is on the mainland, not on Vancouver Island… it felt confusing to non-locals!

Happy reading,
Michelle Ford

Acknowledgements

First and foremost, thank you to my magnificent Kickstarter backers for believing in this project and putting your support behind me. Especially:

T Holmes
Marilyn Hay
Jacquelynn Remery-Pearson
Tracy Popey
Dragon Wytch

A huge thanks to Tristan Williams and Misha Smirnov who graciously volunteered their law enforcement expertise. Any deviations from reality are strictly my own.

My editor, Megan Records, and my beta readers Gillian Brownlee, Steven Shelford, Nadene, and Ashley helped me polish this book into its best possible version.

About the Author

Michelle Ford adores books, cheese, and the West Coast of Canada. Tying these all together in a cozy mystery bundle was a tasty treat she couldn't resist.

Michelle also writes urban fantasy novels under the name Emma Shelford. Visit emmashelford.com to find out more.

Printed in the USA
CPSIA information can be obtained
at www.ICGtesting.com
LVHW041929251223
767391LV00004B/61

9 781989 677483